The Harvesting

The Harvesting

Contents

Prologue

The first alien abduction reports date back to the 1930s but became more widely reported in the 1950s, gaining in recognition through to now.

The most popular reports involve people going in to a trance-like state and finding themselves on board an alien ship, being medically examined.

Most examinations seem to concentrate on the reproductive area with fewer reports stating interest in the brain or upper part of the torso and very few reports have been made regarding the circulatory system and almost none about the cardiovascular system. But all report a loss of time.

Many experts believe experiments have been carried out in the areas of cross-breading to produce hybrids between aliens and humans. In fact, some people believe we are more likely to be of extraterrestrial origins than of Earth, and that other types of earlier man such as *Homo Habilis* and *Homo Erectus* — amongst others — are earlier experiments and aliens did in fact wipe out the dinosaurs knowing that we couldn't simply co-exist.

Many believe if they hadn't, dinosaurs would have eventually evolved in to smaller more intelligent beings and ultimately would have remained the dominant species rather than mammals.

The most popular description of abductors is 'Grey's'. These aliens are said to have three long fingers and large black eyes, a large elongated skull, and grey skin. Hostility varies between reports with some abductees claiming to be treated with compassion; even ending their ordeal with a tour of the ship whilst some report aggressive, even brutal, treatment leaving the abductees with feelings of being raped. Some people suffer from sympathy for the alien, which is seen as Stockholm syndrome whilst others that have been violated suffer from Post Traumatic Stress Disorders. There are very few reports of people over forty being abducted; the trend seems to favour mostly young men and occasionally women in their twenties lending strength to the argument of inter-breeding experiments.

But all of these accounts rely on the abducted being returned to tell their story. What of the people who simply vanish completely, never to be heard from again? Are conspiracies of deals between governments and aliens correct? Allowing them to take as many people as they wish in exchange for technology; the explosion in the late 20th century of new advancements certainly lends weight to the argument.

But what if these 'experiments and returns' are only a planned and controlled way of hiding the real reason behind the abductions? A smoke screen! And if that was the case then what would the real reason be?

Chapter One
The Rain

The rotor blades of the helicopter cut through the cold November air as it made its final approach from the oil fields off the Scottish coast in to Aberdeen airport.

John Andrews had worked the oil fields for seven years and always looked forward to the flight back to the mainland and home.

Settled in his usual seat, the dark grey skies of the afternoon allowed little light through the small curved framed windows; he could see the angled wheel supports and the thick rubber tyre it supported, but beyond that nothing but the infinite greyness of the sky and the foreboding waves of the sea below, which with the exception of the odd splash of white surf, was just as dark and as grey as the sky above them.

Looking forward he could see down the open fuselage and in through the flight deck; the wipers on the pilot's screen endlessly tried to clear the fine drizzle from it and endlessly failed to do so, but he was looking past them, he was looking for the approaching land and he didn't have to wait long before he saw the airport approaching.

He sat back and smiled to himself, this journey home was to be more special than normal. Today was his son's birthday, Mickey would be three today. They had talked last night on the computer using the webcam he had bought him on his last trip home; just seeing his smiling face with his blue eyes and curly blonde hair — which he got from his mother, Samantha — in the three-inch square window on the laptop had made him wish they lived much closer to where he worked, or even better, worked closer to where they lived.

John and his family lived in Hutton Rudby, a small village in the north east of England. They had moved there five years ago; buying a small terraced cottage and renovating it to make what they called, 'The perfect peaceful family home' and they both saw themselves seeing their days out long after Mickey had grown and left to make his own mark on the world.

But this was a long time away and for now, John, Sam and Mickey were living the almost perfect life; the type you see in the adverts put together by marketing executives who want you to believe that buying the products they are pushing this week will give you the idyllic life you crave — that is of course until they work the next account then it will be that product you'll need to have because without it, they will convince you your life could never be perfect!

As the helicopter made its final approach the one-hour flight from the oil field was almost over but he knew he then had an eight-hour drive down the east coast of Scotland and into

England, but at least he wouldn't be on his own; he had his work-mates with him. He turned over his right shoulder and nodded to both of them. Paul Custance and Lee Stokes had joined the oil industry with John, they had worked away together on more than one occasion and in almost every part of the world and whilst John had met Sam and settled down, Paul and Lee had remained firm bachelors, preferring to spend their 'shore' time trying to forget having been away and the fact they have to go away again.

The helicopter bounced down, the thick rubber tyres now taking the weight of it as the lift provided by the huge blades became less as the engines and rotas started to slow eventually, winding down to a whisper, allowing the sound of the rain tapping against the metal fuselage to replace them as the dominant sound.

"You ready for the final leg?" John asked Paul and Lee as he rubbed his eyes and yawned. He was tired, but he had to face the drive, dropping Lee at Newcastle upon Tyne on the way down and finally Paul in to Darlington before his own final leg of the journey.

"Let's get it over with," replied Lee.

The three men climbed down the steps with their kit-bags slung over their shoulders leaning forward and turning their faces away as they guarded themselves against the strong coastal wind that drove the cold rain at them and it seemed straight through them.

The car park wasn't a particularly long walk, at least when they had parked it hadn't seemed so, but the weather had been much warmer and much sunnier.

This band of rain had caught everybody by surprise, even the Met Office hadn't predicted it, and it seemed to cover the whole of the UK, in fact the men that had arrived to relieve John's team had mentioned something about it spreading globally, but John dismissed this as the usual exaggerations people make about the weather, like when the "chance of snow" is mentioned and before you know it everybody will be snowed in for days and we're on the brink of another ice-age, so people start panic-buying, stocking up on water and food, only for the snow to fall and melt all at the same time.

Eventually they reached the Citroen C5, a car they had bought between them to get them there and back, as the car would be parked up for three weeks at a time none of them wanted to bring their own cars up and the room and comfort the big Citroen offered them made it an ideal vehicle for the job it had to do.

Lee took his usual position in the back with Paul in the passenger seat while John took charge in the driver's seat. No actual arrangements or agreements had been made about who should drive and who should sit where, it just seemed to turn out that way, perhaps because John was the oldest and biggest by some margin standing at 6ft2", weighing in at 125kg, Paul and Lee seemed happy to follow him in most situations, and in this case John was happy about this, he wasn't a good passenger; in fact if he could fly the helicopter he would!

The diesel engine fired in to life and instantly the automatic wipers started their own battle to keep the windshield clear of the relentless rain whilst the headlights illuminated the darkened day that had closed in on them and as they did John could make out the fine drops of the sea fret as each one passed through the beams.

Paul checked the clock, 1:37pm.

"Should be home for about half-nine, will Mickey still be up?" he asked.

"I'm sure he will be, with all the sugar and sweets he'll be eating at his birthday party he'll be running around for hours." John replied with an affectionate smile on his face. With that he put the automatic gearbox into drive and pointed the car south for the journey home.

The scenery down the north east coast of Scotland as they headed out of Aberdeen and towards Dundee was as always breathtaking. The mountains on one side with the low clouds rolling over the tops and down in to the valleys and fields below and on the other side the shearing cliffs leading down to the North Sea.

These views always left Paul in awe of what time and the weather can do calving through solid rock and shaping the cliff edges in to shapes and contours that the best sculptors could only wish and dream they were capable of.

After two hours they had passed Dundee and after three hours they had passed through Edinburgh heading south on the A1 towards Berwick and the border with England. The automatic wipers had switched off just before they had reached Edinburgh as the rain had stopped, whilst the climate control kept the car at a warm 22°c, the sky had cleared of the rain that had followed them since leaving the oil fields earlier that day, but the dark menacing clouds still remained.

Just before reaching Lamberton around four hours in to their journey the rain started again and again the wipers started in vein to keep the windscreen clear. This rain seemed different to the driving rain that had followed them until Edinburgh, it seemed to have a purple tint to it. At first John tried to convince himself — even reassure himself — that it was the tinted windows and maybe the darkened skies, but his mind soon threw that explanation out, and whilst part of him wanted to believe it was the tint because that would have made it easy, he knew deep down it wasn't, he knew like all things the easiest explanation, the safest explanation, the one that wouldn't worry him wouldn't be the correct one, but his concentration snapped back when he noticed a residue being left by the wipers as if someone had poured syrup or honey over the screen.

"Notice anything strange about this rain?" he was met by a silence from his travel companions. He looked in his mirror to see Lee asleep, turning to his left Paul looked dazed; he looked like he had taken a blow to his head from a heavyweight boxer and a ref should be counting him out, then a look of pleasure and absolute relaxation swept across his face, "You ok?" John had a concerned tone in his voice. "Paul, Paul, what's wrong?" John let go of the steering wheel with his left hand and shook Paul's leg but as the words came out Paul slipped in to unconsciousness besides him and he realised with dread that Lee wasn't simply asleep, he was in the same condition.

Panic started to set in and as it did he started to feel fatigued, the feeling came on him in an instant; he felt his energy draining away like a battery in a child's toy that that had been left switched on for too long and had started slowing until eventually it simply stopped.

He hit the button for the driver's electric window which instantly lowered, the cooling wind hit his face giving him an instant lift and bringing him momentarily back to an almost full state of awareness. It was then he noticed it; the air, it seemed thick and it had a sour smell about it, burning his nostrils. He pulled his head back into the car, his gag reflex making him reach but he fought the impulse to be sick. Hitting the window switch the glass started to raise and as it did John could feel a euphoria flow over him as if all the worries in his life — everything that had made him sad as a child or cross as an adult — had simply been lifted away from him, he felt himself starting to smile, his hands relaxed and fell off the steering wheel and as they did John too slipped in to a state of unconsciousness.

His right foot slipped off the accelerator pedal and the car started to slow 50, 45, 40...35. As it reached 35mph the road turned to the right but the car didn't, it smashed through the low wooden fence sending splinters and shrapnel of wood in all directions; most of them hitting the car as it passed through the gap it had created.

As the runaway car started down the incline its speed started to increase 35, 37...40mph, the car burst through a barrier of bushes that lined the bottom of the hill engulfing the car.

Now only the tracks left by the tyres in the soft wet grass and the smashed fence back at the top of the hill gave any clue that the car had recently passed through. As the shrubs and bushes battered and protested against the glass and metal work of the body, the front came in to contact with the large tree. The car started to crumple instantly and as it did the air bags deployed, the three occupants — unaware of what was happening to them — were flung forward by the momentum that still carried them inside the car.

The seat belts immediately snagged around them compressing their chests and holding them fast; their internal organs continued to travel forward slamming against their muscle walls and rib cages, their arms and legs carried on.

Lee's smacked against the back of the thick velour driver's seat, John and Paul's limbs flayed against the dashboard and controls of the car. The air bags, now fully deployed, took the final forward motion and energy away from them before they deflated. As they did the tree broke through the plastic and metal protection offered by the bumper and cross beams of the car, the radiator was the first to be breached, steam erupted as the pressurised water hit the atmosphere and instantly boiled sending jets of super heated steam up through the smashed bonnet.

The next to go was the battery container; the tree trunk had passed with ease through the left-side of the engine compartment, the battery smashed against the thick wooden trunk, the plastic body shattered releasing a waterfall of acid, as it did the car raised its back wheels off the ground in one last attempt to keep moving forward, but the tree stood firm and it came to a complete stop, the rear wheels smashed back down to the ground sending the unconscious passengers back from their forward position into their seats.

Now in almost complete silence with only the sound of the strangely coloured and smelling rain tapping on the twisted body shell and shattered glass, the car vanished, camouflaged completely by the shrubbery it had breached on its way to the tree; the steam from the smashed radiator eventually dispersed, and as the last of the battery power ebbed away the outside lights dimmed and blinked off, the dashboard displays went blank and the last thing on the car to draw power was the clock and as it eventually became blank it displayed 5:37pm.

11:37am New York

Brad was on his way to yet another meeting, yet another chance to stand in front of his line manager with his measured suit and his smooth shaven image and present yet another sales report.

He would brag about how well his department is doing under his stewardship, and how no-one else could deliver the results he can. He would tell Jennie how she made the right choice in hiring him over all the other candidates and how one day he would earn her admiration.

The routine went around in his head as the elevator counted up the floors from his department on the 5th floor to the meeting rooms on the 18th — the higher the number floor in this company the more important you were, until of course you reached the 32nd floor where the VPs sit and the 32nd floor was Brad's target.

He wanted the respect he saw in peoples' eyes when the VPs entered the building, and the special reserved parking he would walk past on the way to his 'outdoor' spot. One day he would have the Aston Martin or Lexus parked in there, but not today, no today he had to nail this presentation. Sales had not been going to plan. Brad's department was falling behind on the promises he said he could deliver, but of course he had a patsy, someone else he could blame for the short comings, he had it all figured out and there was no way he would take the fall, not today and not by Jennie's doing!

The elevator door opened and Brad was met by a site that forced him to stop dead between the elevator doors. At the large reception desk in front of him that proudly displayed the company name and tag line *"Asclepius Solutions...Developing cures for tomorrow's world"*. Laura the receptionist, that had always welcomed him with a smile and a professional courtesy, lay across the desk; the phone headset laid discarded, he could see that she must have fallen forward hitting her head against the large solid wood desk; as she did knocking the headset off and sending it sprawling away from her. At first he thought she had collapsed, he stepped out of the elevator doors moving towards her to offer what help he could, then he noticed everybody else, everybody he knew laying on the floor.

Some looked peaceful as if they had intentionally lay down and made themselves comfortable before going to sleep. Others, Jennie included, didn't look so peaceful, she was laid in a heap on the floor, her legs straddled across the chair she had obviously been sitting on before she had slumped to the side. Her normally neat blonde hair covered her face and the laptop she had been using when she had slipped now lay beside her, its screen still waiting patiently for the next command.

Brad felt a sense of panic at first; he couldn't make sense of what he was seeing. Paranoia started to take over, was this a company wide joke, just at the point when he was about to lose control and break down would everybody jump up and shout, "Surprise"? or could it be worse, could it be some sort of 'new thinking' test to see how he worked under extreme pressure?

He had heard of these new management techniques but nothing this excessive, but then he noticed the windows and what was outside; the purple rain that soaked them and the thick smearing ooze that ran behind the raindrops; he started to make his way back to the elevator, walking backwards in slow small deliberate steps, but Brad didn't make the return journey, with his left leg inside the elevator and his right leg outside he collapsed. His carefully prepared presentation scattered around him, his laptop smashed against the steel runners of the door mounts sending bits of printed circuit boards across the highly-polished reception floor. His eyes focused for a split second on the ceiling of the elevator's interior; a faint and very polite voice caught his concentration, "Please stand clear of the doors," and then he too fell asleep.

1:37am Brisbane Queensland Australia

Aiden and Brooke were heading back down the Brisbane River from the mouth of Mouton Bay when the rain started.

The purple foul-smelling rain drifted in like a fog at first; the thick syrupy solution soon soaked Aiden who was in the wheel house of the little fishing boat. Below deck in the small cramped galley Brooke prepared the freshly-caught fish.

Suddenly and without warning the boat turned aggressively. Brooke tried to steady himself and as he did he heard a dull thud from the deck above.

"Jesus, Aiden what the hell ya doing?"

He made his way up to the wheel house, at first he couldn't see Aiden, he couldn't see much at all, the purple rain had enclosed their little boat completely and the eerie mist that accompanied the rain had swallowed what little moon light there was.

Brooke moved further out of the doorway, "Aiden? Aiden where the hell are you mate?"

Now he could see Aiden, at least he could see his leg, hanging over the side.

"Shit!"

Brooke raced over and started to pull Aiden back on to the boat. Aiden had succumbed to the rain, he had fallen to his left, spinning the wheel of the little boat and as he did he stumbled over the side catching his leg in the netting they had used to catch their fish. His head and upper body had gone under the water, dragging him like a buoy down the side of the boat. As Brooke tried to pull him in he felt himself starting to lose his concentration, a feeling of well-being and contentment washed over him as the river had washed over Aiden. He let go of his friend who slipped head first back in to the water still held by the net.

Brooke's weight and the position he had taken

to save his friend took him over the side, with a splash no-one else would hear. Brooke disappeared and the little boat carried on its journey; its small navigation lights only just penetrating the purple rain that now covered the entire continent of Australia.

6:37pm Paris France: Europe

Like the UK, Australia and America before it, Paris was not expecting rain that day, and it certainly wasn't expecting the purple sticky rain that now covered the globe; and like everywhere else everybody in Paris was asleep — a deep dreamless sleep brought about by the purple rain and mist that had enveloped the world. Destruction soon followed the sleep and was everywhere, the lucky ones had been sitting or even just walking or cycling when the rain came or in their offices or homes.

The people in cars, boats, on trains and in planes had not been so lucky. Motorways were a scene of carnage; multiple collisions as driver after driver had fallen asleep and allowed their cars, trucks or buses to simply collide at whatever speed they were doing in to other moving or stationary vehicles. Trains careered into stations, de-railing and wiping clear complete platforms of sleeping commuters, with the ease you wipe an insect from your arm. Some trains collided with others, high speed trains — hitting goods trains at speeds approaching 200mph, whole carriages smashed beyond recognition and with them the unfortunate sleeping travellers inside.

Airports faired no better, planes on take-off crashed back to earth whilst planes on their final approaches smashed into the terminals or other planes waiting in turn to taxi out. Some planes circled on autopilot, keeping themselves in the air until of course the fuel ran out and then they too tumbled down adding to the hundreds of thousands who died whilst in their slumber.

Across the world ships collided, in the busiest shipping lanes in the world, the English Channel, ferries carrying holiday makers, business men and goods vehicles smashed in to larger container ships; by the time the last of the ships had ran in to each other the shipping lane was littered with capsized and crippled vessels — some spilling their cargo into the sea, some managing to hold on to it, but all of them destined to sink, destined to disappear beneath the waves and all of them would take their sleeping cargo with them.

Ferries that had been on their final approach had smashed in to the docks, or run over smaller yachts pushing them under their hulls along with the sleeping captains and crew. Other ships carried on until they hit land, large ships strewed along the coast line — the engines still running as if trying to push the ships further on to the land and safety. But by now there was no safety in the sky on land or at sea, the purple rain was everywhere, the earth from space had lost its distinctive blue and green, now it appeared as a shimmering purple cloud.

Chapter Two
Tom McKinley

John was the first to wake up, his eyes opened slowly, still not fully conscious but not completely unconscious. He wasn't sure where he was; was he still dreaming or had he woken up? He felt unsure, confused, his head felt thick — somehow fuzzy as if he was floating. He felt the same we all do when have fallen asleep in front of the TV. The pictures are the first to go then the sound, ten-minutes into the movie or documentary we wanted to see, then with a start we wake up to the phone ringing or to someone knocking on the door. Our senses struggle at first then flood back over us but we don't quite know when or where we are, we feel confused, dazed — even stunned and that's exactly how John was feeling now.

He rubbed his eyes and slowly found his senses coming back on line as his brain started to re-boot. He looked around and started to recognise the dashboard in front of him, the now limp air bags hung out of the steering wheel and dashboard, some of the sticky rain had leaked in through the shattered windscreen and leaving stains on the grey plastics. Dapples of sunlight were splattered around the car's interior; from what light could penetrate the thick hedges and foliage that had kept the car hidden, and a soft warm breeze filtered in through the gap between his door and frame of the car's twisted body.

His seat belt still felt tight against his chest and through the shattered windshield he could make out the outline of the crumpled bonnet and the large tree that had stopped the *out of control* car in its tracks, and whilst they didn't know it, ultimately from driving off the edge of a cliff and in to the North Sea one hundred fifty feet below.

He reached around and pushed the red release button for seat belt, the metal fastener clicked and the tension was instantly taken off his chest, he felt relief and pulled the belt around him, he breathed in deeply only to feel a sharp intense pain rush around his body, he winced sharply through closed teeth, he was sore, very sore, and lifting his white T-shirt up he could see why; the bruising around his abdomen caused by the belt as it had held him back from travelling straight through the windshield and in to the tree was extensive, large blue and black-*purplish* patches covered his torso like a patchwork quilt. John turned to his left, Paul was starting to come round too and like John he was confused and dazed at first but slowly he started to remember where he was, but as all three of them became fully conscious none of them could remember the crash or how and when they had left the road.

They weren't sure how long they had been sitting in the broken car. John spoke first, none of them could really think that clearly.

"Can you all move, do you have any broken bones?" he asked.

"No, we seem to be okay, just sore and little bemused I guess," Lee replied.

John relaxed back in to his seat and turned to Paul, "Pass my phone, it's in the glove box."

Paul reached in and found John's phone and passed it to him. He watched as John slid the keypad up and then stopped and stared at it with a look of confusion, "What's up? Paul asked.

"It's dead, I charged it before we left, it should have been good for two or three days on standby."

"Might have been the crash, try pushing the power button."

John turned to Paul, "I have! It's dead! Try yours."

Paul reached in to his jeans pocket and pulled his phone out, holding it up in front of him he turned to John, "Just the same, mine's dead too."

"And mine," Lee added and then continued, "I charged mine in here I plugged in to the cigar lighter in the back, it was charging while you were driving it should be good for a few days yet!"

John turned round as far as he could in his seat

to face Lee, he looked at him and a strange —
and for Lee — unsettling look came over John's
face. John's gaze moved around Lee's face; his
eyes looked puzzled and Lee started to feel
very uncomfortable by his stare.

"John what are you looking at?"

John didn't reply, he just kept staring,
studying his friend, someone he had know now
for twelve years, and without doubt the one in
the group that kept himself the best-groomed.
Lee was always the clean shaven one, the one
who kept his hair perfect even when working
on the rigs in the North Sea and John knew
without a doubt in his mind that Lee would
had shaved and showered this morning before
they left the oil fields as he always did, and that
was why John was staring at him.

"You did your usual shave and preening
routine this morning Lee before we left?"

"What? What the fuck you on about John?
What's he talking about, Paul?"

Lee turned to Paul to find him with the same
look as John.

"What's going on?"

Lee's concern was starting to take hold, he
darted forward between them reaching for the
interior mirror; grabbing hold he twisted it
round, "Jesus!"

John turned back in his seat taking the mirror
from Lee, he turned it back towards himself,
"I'm just the same," both men then turned to

Paul, "So are you," John said. Paul moved his hand slowly up to his face and started to rub his chin. He turned to John, "Just exactly how long have we been here?" All three men had a substantial growth of stubble and all three men had been clean shaven when they had started their journey home, which to them was no more than a few hours ago.

"I don't know but this along with the dead phones tells me it's been more than a couple of hours. I think we should get back to the road and flag down some help," John replied.

The three men pushed the doors of the Citroen open, battling against the thick bushes; they pushed through the hedgerow until they came to the grassy hill the car had raced down; retracing the now almost invisible tyre tracks until they reached the gap in the fence the car had made on its way through. Bits of wood still lay in the middle of the road. John stood and looked both ways along the road then turned to Paul, "Why do you think this wood is still here? I mean, if another car had driven over it or even the large trucks that use this road it would have broken up and splintered."

Paul just shook his head, he was still trying to become fully awake and questions that large were just too much for his brain to cope with right now. The sky was a clear blue, not a cloud blotted it anywhere, and it was warm, unusually warm for this time of the year.

"Which way?" asked Lee.

John stood for a while and looked both ways again and then turned, "North." He said this with the usual assurance that had made Paul and Lee follow him around the world on different work contracts, he continued, "We head back North, Burnmouth is about four miles that way, there's that Inn we keep passing, you know, near the one that burned down a few years ago."

"I know the one," Paul replied.

John continued, "If we go there we can call for help and find out what day it is, and then call home, Sam will be worried."

The three men started the walk to Burnmouth, they felt sure they would see a car or truck or even a motorbike, something, someone, but they saw nothing until they reached the inn, its car park was half full and through the windows they could see the table lights, even in the strong sunlight.

"What did I tell you?" John said with a growing optimism. They crossed the road and entered the inn to find it completely empty, not a soul was in the place but everything else that should have been there was: coats hanging by the doorway, food on the tables, some only half-eaten, some not touched, drinks on the bar and money; one of the tills still open and the jukebox played its random tunes destined to forever circulate the songs on its hard drive until the power gave out or someone paid it to play their particular choice, and right now it played Genesis *'I can't dance'*.

The three men walked further into the empty inn, the large flat screen TV that hung on the mock fireplace now just displayed a blue screen with a never-ending message window moving up and down the screen in a random pattern; 'No signal check input'. John headed for the bar and looked over the top of it whilst Paul and Lee headed for the swing doors that entered the kitchen. Paul pushed on the door that said 'Enter', leaning through it he carefully peered inside and like the bar and restaurant it too was empty. Lee turned to John, "What's going here? it's really staring to freak me out!"

John just shook his head, it was the first time Lee had seen John look so hesitant, so unsure of what to do next: He stood motionless, staring back at Lee and then breaking his pause he spoke, "I don't know what this is, but I know what we have to do, let's get some food and water, take one of the cars that's outside and head home, maybe it's confined to Scotland, maybe when we get to the English border there'll be police road blocks, maybe even the Army."

Paul came back from the kitchen. "It's the same in there, nothing, nobody, just food on the counters waiting to be served." Then he stopped and looked around, and both men could see a change in his expression and it was one that filled them with dread at what he would say next...

"How long does it take for food to go bad, very bad?"

"I know bread can keep for few days, why?"

Paul pointed to one of the untouched meals on the table closest to them, "That's why, that looks like it's been there for a long time to me."

John and Lee followed his finger to the meal he pointed at, the burger and chips that had once offered some traveller a hardy meal before they had continued North or even South had long since gone cold. The fat from the burger had congealed on the plate forming a thick white moat around the now green mouldy bread bun, the cheese slice that sat on top of it had mould of its own now consuming it and the Ice Berg lettuce that was the only healthy thing on the plate had turned its leaves up and turned brown, the fries had fared no better with time, now curled and mouldy. The whole meal looked like one of the dares some Z-list celebrity would have to eat in some god awful show to win a prize or real food for the other contestants.

John turned back to Paul, "Did you see a phone in the kitchen?"

"Yes I did, just inside the doorway."

"Okay, you two find car keys, anything will do so long as it will get us South and out of this bloody nightmare, I'm going to try the phone and call Sam."

John headed for the kitchen, Paul started with the coats, still hanging by the door, while Lee headed over to the tables, looking for keys that had been placed on the table by the diners who had never got the chance to finish their meals or drinks, but there were none. It seemed even this far from towns and cities people were just nervous about leaving keys in their unattended jackets and coats or even next to them on the tables.

John came back out of the kitchen and Lee turned to see him, he had to ask if he'd been able to reach Sam, but even as the words left his mouth he could tell by the look on John's face that he hadn't.

"Any luck getting through?"

John just shook his head and replied with two words: "No answer."

He looked flattened but then continued, "Any keys?"

"None," Lee replied.

"Wherever these people went to they took their keys with them."

Paul interrupted both men, "But not their phones or wallets!"

John turned to face him and Paul continued, "Look all around, on the tables, floors, everywhere, it's like everyone left their phone behind along with their wallets!"

"ID!" Lee added.

"What?"

"It's not their wallets and phones they've left behind it's their ID, the phones have all their contacts for friends, family, and themselves you know...diaries etc, these new phones do everything and it's all kept in one handy place, lose that and you lose everything, and the wallets have their driving licences and bank cards, everything that can be traced."

John looked puzzled. "But that doesn't make sense, if you took a pub full of people you wouldn't leave stuff behind to help ID who there were."

"Well, you would if who they were didn't matter once you took them."

A daunting feeling fell across the three of them with Lee's last remark, and all three of them felt that sickening harrowing feeling we all get when we convince ourselves the worst has either just happened or is about to.

"FUCK!" John shouted, he turned and hammered his fist down on to the bar counter, clenching both fists he rested his hands on it and bowed his head down.

"What's happening? What is this?"

Paul walked up and sat on one of the tall stools next to him. "Look, there must be some keys here, we haven't checked the staff lockers yet, one of the cars out there must belong to someone from the staff and if they left in a big enough hurry not to take their cars I bet they didn't empty their lockers either, we'll get you home tonight big man and then you'll see that Sam and Mickey are fine." John relaxed his shoulders, "Okay, you look through the lockers. Lee, put some sandwiches together, the bread in the fridges and freezers should still be okay, and the electrics on which means the microwaves will work and grab some bottles of water, at least that should be alright, I'm going to the toilet."

Paul headed through the *'staff only'* door and Lee went back into the kitchen whilst John entered the toilets. Standing at a urinal he stared into the long mirror that stretched the full width of the wall. As he did the door on the third stall from the left — or was it the right? (John could never figure out the whole reverse mirror thing), started to move, slowly at first, hardly noticeable, in fact just enough for John to question whether it was moving or not but as he watched it, it moved again and then it started to gather pace. John finished what he was doing and fastened himself back up before spinning round to face the door head on as the gap between it and the thin frame it fastened to became large, the metal angled hinges which were designed to make the door open unless it was being held or it was locked from the inside started to creek and groan as the dry metal rubbed against itself. John looked around for anything he could use as a weapon, he had no idea who was behind the door, maybe it was someone responsible for what was going on and if it was, was that person friendly? had everybody been evacuated for their own good or against their will? As these questions raced through his mind the gap in the door widened. John's heart began to race, his adrenaline started to rush around his body and his mouth became dry, so very dry.

John is a big man but he hadn't been in a fight since he was at school. What if this person was a trained killer? What if he had a knife or a gun? Shit! a gun, more thoughts rushed at him. Sam and Mickey; if he were to die here now he'd never know what this is or even if they're safe. His mind came to rest and one thought alone pushed through all the other jumbles of panic and hysteria that had chassed around his body and that thought was the one his old physical ed teacher had drummed in to them during rugby practice over and over again. He could hear his old teacher, standing on the cold wet field of Stainsby Modern Comprehensive; the rain pelting them and wind driving against them his voice almost making the wind yield to him whilst he shouted down field to a young John who stood with the ball in his hands: "Andrews, attack is the best from of defence! Now run, lad, *RUN!*"

John snapped back, he looked at the now half-open door, he took shape, the one that was drilled in to him before running with the other forwards on the rugby pitch and he charged the door. He hit it at full pace, at least what was full pace now which was less than it had been all those years ago. He burst through it knocking whoever was behind it down, wedging them between the now fully open door and the false wall of the cubicle.

"Who are you?" John shouted with the most authoritive voice he could muster in between the shots of adrenaline and nerves; which were starting to take a hold of him now that his mind and body had caught up with his actions.

"Please stop, please, my name is Tom McKinley. I was in here doing…well, you know, and then I woke up and heard you outside. I didn't know who you were."

John stood over the small balding man who was now cowering on the floor. He had an ill-fitting *off-the-peg* suit on and was holding a mobile phone in his free hand whilst the other was holding on to the edge of the door for life itself.

"So you have no idea either what's going on?" John asked.

"What do you mean what's going on? I just nodded off, you woke me when you came in."

John released the door that was still pinning Tom against the wall and held out his hand to help him up.

"So you have no idea what's going on at all?"

Tom stood up and stepped out of the cubicle. "You keep saying what's going on, but I've told you I came in here, fell asleep a few minutes ago and you woke me up, now if you will please excuse me I'll head back to my table, my wife will wondering where I am."

John stepped to one side, too weary and tired to try and convince this fussy little man of what he had seen, he decided to let him head back out in to restaurant and see for himself.

John followed behind as Tom walked in to the now completely empty bar where he stopped dead in his tracks.

John walked up beside him. "See, all gone...everybody gone!"

Tom turned to John, "But I don't understand, this was full a few minutes ago."

As he spoke Paul came back through the 'staff only' door. "No keys in there either J..." but he stopped immediately when he saw Tom standing next to John and then continued, "thank Christ we're not alone." He rushed over to where Tom stood and pushed out his hand ready to shake Tom's. "I'm Paul, so glad to see someone else, do you know what's happened or where everybody has gone?" Tom didn't get a chance to answer.

"No, he has no idea I found him in one of the cubicles in the toilets, he..." John stopped and looked at Paul, a look for reluctance appeared on his face, the type of look you see just before someone gives you some bad news that they really don't want, he sighed and continued, "he fell asleep as well, he was waking up when we came in here."

Tom butted in and protested, "I told you I've only been asleep a short while — minutes if that!"

John turned to face him, "Really, look at your phone Tom."

Tom turned the tiny phone to face him, its shiny piano black case shone in the strong sunlight that came in through the large corner windows, but as with their phones its screen was blank, dead, it displayed nothing, even as Tom tried in vein to bring it out of standby the little phone had given up, its battery long since exhausted.

"I don't understand, it charges while I'm driving. I had the kit fitted so it would, they told me in the shop…"

John interrupted him, "They weren't lying Tom, but you've been in there a lot longer than you think and so were we. I bet you were clean shaven this morning as well?"

Tom turned to look in to one of the large mirrors behind the bar, "Oh god! what the hell is this, am I dreaming?"

John turned to Paul, "No keys?"

"No, none, all the lockers were locked, it is like everybody just stopped what they were doing and walked out..." he paused, "after dropping their phones and ID!"

John turned back to Tom, who was now up against the bar looking at his unshaven reflection, "How long was I in there? This is four or five days' growth."

"I know how we can tell." Paul spun round, the excitement in his voice raised up. "The tills are still on, they always show the time and date."

Paul rushed over to the bar and climbed over it, knocking over half-drunken bottles and glasses of soft drinks in the process, sending them spinning on the floor. He hit the keyboard and instantly the little square monitor came to life. John watched as his face turned an ashen grey; all the anticipation and optimism washed away from it in an instant and John felt sick to his stomach.

"What is it?"

Paul looked up, "It's the date."

"Well?" John demanded.

"It says December 12th."

John stood perfectly still, almost statuesque.

"Repeat that," Tom muttered.

"December 12th."

Paul rushed to the next till and repeated the procedure to bring the little screen to life.

"This one says the same."

Tom sat, almost falling back into the chair next to him.

"Lynne?"

John turned, "What?"

"Lynne, my wife, we were on our way back from Edinburgh, a friend's wedding, we stopped to eat, there, I left her sitting there." He pointed to the table that had the un-eaten and rotten beef burger on it they had looked at when they had come in.

Paul clambered back over the bar, the energy he had had when he first went over the bar had been sucked clean out of him, and it dawned on them there and then that they had been asleep for over two weeks, cocooned in their broken and smashed car in a state of slumber whilst Tom had fallen off the toilet and come to rest off the floor between the toilet bowl and the frame of the door. By nothing more than chance he was invisible to anyone walking in, in the same way the bushes and shrubs had hidden the Citroen from above.

John, Paul and Tom sat at the table Tom had sat at with his wife Lynne, leaning back in the chair he had occupied before going to the toilet he pushed the plate of rotten food away from him and sighed deeply, with a sad look on his little round face he pushed his small round spectacles further up his nose and looked up at John.

"So why were you passing?"

John was playing with the salt shaker, he had his hands loosely closed around it and was passing it from hand to hand. He looked up at Tom and carefully placed the shaker back in the middle of the table, "We are..." he stopped then started again... "we were on our way down from the North Sea oil fields on our way home, one minute we were driving along, then…" He paused again... "I don't remember, then, I know we must have fallen asleep because I know I woke up and our car was against a tree at the bottom of a hill. We climbed out and walked here looking for help and found..." He stopped again but this time Tom interrupted him, "Found me?"

John and Paul smiled.

"Yes Tom, we found you."

Tom looked a little more relaxed, he sat forward clasping his hands together, he reminded John of someone who was about to prey.

"What's your next plan? Now that it seems there is no help."

"Well, Paul was looking for car keys when I found you, I think if we get to the border with England I'm hopeful there will be people and more importantly: answers."

"You think this is confined to Scotland?" Tom asked.

"I don't know but it's a good enough guess for now." Tom looked thoughtful, sucking on his bottom lip, a smile spread slowly across his face.

"I have that Landrover Discovery in the car park I can take you, I need to find Lynne, if people were evacuated she maybe there looking for me."

John and Paul nodded, "Thank you, Tom." John said.

"It'll certainly speed the journey up rather than walking." Tom looked pleased he could help. John got the impression he liked to help.

"He's one of life's helpers and all-round good guy." He thought to himself.

"So, should the three of us go?" Tom asked.

"Three?" Paul replied.

Tom nodded and counted round the little group, "One, two, three."

"No, there's one more, Lee," Paul replied.

"Where is Lee? It shouldn't take this long to knock a few sandwiches together." John said.

As the words left his mouth a loud clatter came from the kitchen, it was the unmistakable sound of stainless steel pots and pans being tipped up and hurled. The three men sat at the little round table turned to look at the kitchen together, and as they did the swing doors were flung open.

Chapter Three
The Rejects

The three men focused intently on the kitchen door as it swung violently open and then back again; swinging in ever-decreasing arcs until it almost came to a stop. Tom rose from his seat, "What was that?" his voice had a concerned tone to it, even frightened, the type of tone you hear coming from a child who is convinced beyond any doubt that there is a monster under their bed and even though you've looked for them and proved beyond all doubt that's it's empty under there *(apart from the usual broken toys and orange peels)* once your out the door a hand will slowly appear from around the side of the bed and drag the terrified child under — never to return!

"I don't know." John sounded different to Tom, not scared or frightened by the monster in the kitchen which Tom now imagined it must be. John sounded anxious, he sounded concerned for his friend Lee who he knew was in there making sandwiches and collecting the cold bottled drinks. Tom started to move forward but Paul grabbed his wrist, pulling him back a little. "Hang on, Tom," he said. Tom looked down at him surprised by the concern his new friend had shown, and he wanted to smile, just a little acknowledgment of what he had done but Paul was looking straight ahead, they all were and then again suddenly the door flew open, but this time it didn't get the chance to recoil back, this time a figure emerged from the kitchen. A hand held the top of the saloon-shaped door wide open and the figure rounded from the back of it standing square on to them. John squinted, trying to focus his eyes on the shape that stood with its back to the large corner windows causing the brilliantly bright day to silhouette it. What John could make out was that it was a man, his head bowed down and his legs set apart, the arm that wasn't holding on to the door hung away at an angle from his side. It reminded him of a cowboy gun slinger who was ready to draw to settle some argument over a girl or land or even a cow! The three men watched as the figure twitched, his legs seemed to spasm while he stood and his free arm jerked and shook, his head seemed to convulse back and forth and from side to side they were small movements; very small in fact but also very violent. Gradually Paul came to recognise the figure that now stood before them.

"Lee? Lee, is that you? Jesus it is! What's wrong? What's happened?" As Paul stood up from his chair bringing him next to Tom, who still stood fixed to the spot his fight or flight response still deciding which to do, Lee started to raise his head in a vague shuddering manner.

As he did they could hear clicks and grunts coming from him "What did you say, mate?" Paul asked him. He took a step closer but this time it was Tom that took hold of Paul's wrist and held it firm. Lee's head was now fully raised and still his body twitched and convulsed and then they saw his face, his eyes were red, blood shot, bruised and swollen. His face looked pale and drawn and his lips were a thick dull red and inflated. Slowly he raised his upper lip, at first the three men thought he was starting to smile as if it was some sort of bad taste practical joke and that his face was covered with stuff he'd found in the kitchen, but he didn't smile, he drew his lip back over his teeth and started to snarl at them. Saliva ran from his mouth down onto his chin dripping onto his clean blue T-shirt. The clicks and grunts gave way to a low rumbling growl, the spasms and jerks became more and more violent. He let go of the kitchen door and it swung immediately back away from him, his free arm now raised and as it did it started to point directly at them, the snarl turned in to a smile, but it wasn't a pleasant friendly smile, this was a *"I'm coming for you"* smile. Tom started to back away, still holding Paul's wrist, Lee now made a step forward, his head still held high; he glared at them; the growls becoming more repetitive and deeper, resonating in the back of his throat, his legs moved awkwardly towards them. John stood and moved back away from the little round table with Paul and Tom.

Still growling, still half-snarling and half-smiling, Lee moved another step closer towards them. John stepped across in front of Paul and Tom. Raised his hands showing Lee his palms like a policeman on traffic duty trying to stop oncoming traffic. "Lee, just stop there, what's wrong?" He said in the calmest voice he could muster given the circumstances and how he was feeling. Lee cocked his head from side to side like a dog would upon hearing an unusual sound, but still he marched forwards toward them. John stepped a little further forward still gesturing with his hands for him to stop. "Lee, stop there please, don't come any closer." But Lee did and as he did the three of them could see more of him as the light once behind him now shifted around to the side of him. His skin seemed discoloured, it had a yellowish tint to it, the veins that ran around him supplying blood to his muscles and everywhere that needed it seemed to be standing on edge and were a vivid red colour, almost purple, his hair seemed matted somehow and it was missing in patches as if he had tore at it pulling clumps out with his bare hands. The bare scalp was the same yellowish colour as the rest of him. But as he got closer it was the eyes that they found the most disturbing, the once friendly glint in his blue eyes that had always been there was gone. Now they seemed empty, full of hate and anger, and aggression in the eyes you would see in a rabid dog before it attacked. More growls more clicks came as he took another unsteady shaky step then he stopped!

Paul and Tom, still behind John, stopped backing away and John lowered his hands. Lee was now only 10 feet from them still shaking and still twitching looking at the three of them, moving his blooded gaze from one to the other then he stopped and his gaze fixed on Tom. His lips curled again and his eyes squinted.

"Lee, this is the last warning buddy, stay there!"

John's voice had now become sharper. Paul imagined it would be the voice he would use at home to stop Mickey from doing something he shouldn't or even start him doing something he should.

John turned his head to face Paul and Tom behind him

"I think he's in some sort of trance, he seems to be calming down."

But as he spoke his words were shaken from him by the instant commotion that followed. Lee screamed, it wasn't a scream you hear a fan shouting at a concert or sports event in support and joy, it was a scream of pain — even death, but it wasn't Lee's pain, it was aimed at Tom; it was a battle cry designed for one thing to strike terror in to the heart of his victim and Lee had decided that his first victim would be Tom.

He sprang forward, his body still moving in stiff violent actions and he was quick, much faster than the three stunned and confused men had thought he could be.

Within seconds he was on John, he pushed past him catching him off balance and off guard. Tom moved back as quick as he could, his heart beating in his chest, fear washed over him taking his breath like a bucket of cold water on a hot day, "Lynne," was all he could say. His hands raised as if to fend off his attacker as Lee moved closer.

Tom now backed up against the juke box which now played 'Hotel California' and readied himself for the inevitable onslaught. His eyes closed, his mouth curled with fear, his heart-pounding sweat ran out of every pour and he repeated over and over, "Lynne," but nothing came, he knew even with Lee's jerky movements he should have been on him by now. He imagined — only vividly — what he would have done but nothing happened and then he heard the thump. Tom slowly opened his eyes to see Lee lying on the floor at his feet, blood ran freely from a tear in the side of his head, his body still convulsing. Tom looked up at Paul who was looking down on him and in his right hand he held a blooded bar stool, he looked in shock, he had hit his friend hard,

hard enough to knock him out but not to kill.

Tom's hands came down from across his face, still shaking with fear, but they were no longer needed to guard him. "Thank you."

Paul turned to face him and dropped the stool.

"He was my friend, we went everywhere together, we did everything...why would he attack you? Why would he look like that?"

Lee started to click again, his hands started to move, curling up then relaxing.

"I think we should move!" John shouted from where he was standing. "He's only out and when he comes round I think we'll need more than that stool."

Paul turned to face John, "We leave him here?"

"What do you think we should do? Talk to him? you saw the way he looked and sounded."

"He's right," Tom interrupted. "I think he's gone. I don't think he's Lee anymore."

Paul sighed in defeat and looked at his friend still laying, still clicking and still twitching.

Tom took the keys for his Discovery out of his pocket. "Should we?" Tom gestured.

"What about food?" Paul asked.

John turned to face Paul and Tom and pointed South.

"The border is only a few miles away, if this is confined to Scotland there will be food there, and anyway do you want to go into the kitchen? That's where Lee was!"

Paul shook his head, "But what if this isn't confined to Scotland? what if it's in England, Wales — hell, everywhere and we leave with no food."

"Don't worry, there's a supermarket in Berwick, we can fill up there."

Tom stepped over Lee's still shuddering legs, "Can we just leave now?" he asked and again pointed to the exit.

John held out an open arm for Paul, as if to guide him past his friend and out of the inn.

The day was in its last few hours but the light outside was still bright and still too warm for December. They reached Tom's dark green Discovery and climbed aboard. Tom started the big diesel engine and drove out of the car park heading South. As they pulled onto the main road Paul turned in the back seat to look back at the inn and the place he had left his friend — or what his friend had become — and as they turned the corner and the inn disappeared from sight he thought he saw the main entrance door start to open.

The silence seemed to last an eternity as the Landrover travelled along the now deserted road. The main road heading South towards England would normally be full of businessmen travelling home or holiday makers with their caravans heading to the Highlands or even large trucks.

John would always complain about how a lot of it is still single carriageway and that if it had been in the South it would have been two or three lanes now but not today, today John sat as quietly as Paul and Tom; only the constant sound of the diesel engine pulling them along and the rumbling of the tyres stopped the absolute silence.

John had tried the radio almost as soon as they had left but like the TV in the inn, it too gave no information, just the hiss of static and a *'No service'* display on the little LCD screen.

Outside, the bright blue sky was now starting to give way to the night and like the day, no clouds were hanging over them. The Moon had already started to show even before the sun had given up its space and they could already feel the temperature starting to change from the unusually warm day to a usually cold winter's night.

They passed the gap in the fence that their car had made on its way down the hill. Paul looked at it as they passed by it, not even the tyre tracks were visible now and he wondered how long the smashed Citroen would sit hidden amongst the hedges and bushes that had camouflaged them before anybody found it, or whether anybody ever would.

There were some signs of traffic, or at least it had been once-upon-a-time. The cars and trucks they did pass had long been deserted and left exactly where they had stopped; some parked neatly in rows as they had stopped, pulling up in traffic jams before their occupants had fallen asleep and in front of them the inevitable carnage of the smashed glass and the twisted metal of cars and trucks that hadn't been so lucky. These were the ones that had still been travelling when their drivers had succumbed and had only stopped when they had hit something bigger than they were.

As Tom weaved the Landrover through the wrecks until he found clear road again Paul noticed some of them still had their passengers; these hadn't been evacuated or taken — or whatever it was that had caused everyone to disappear — but the ones that were left were charred and black, almost melted into the frame of the seats they had slept in while the fires that had burst out and burnt out of control following the crashes had engulfed them. But all of them were in the same position. All of them looked as though they had been asleep when the fires had started and he felt sure, or at least he had convinced himself, that they hadn't felt a thing while they had burned along with their cars, but what did distress him more than the burnt bodies was that the same pattern followed here as it had with the inn. Mobile phones and wallets littered the deserted carriageway, as with the fate of the people at the inn. Whatever had happened to the people in these cars any form of ID or ability to make contact had been deliberately left behind. He didn't know if John and Tom had noticed but if they had they too had decided not to say anything.

The Landrover climbed over the centre reservations and embankments with ease to find a way through the latest blockade of more smashed cars. They noticed one almost completely crushed by an articulated truck at the front of this particular crash scene and whilst there was blood stains on the road, no doubt from the unfortunate sleeping driver, the body had disappeared with everyone else.

As the road opened up again the sun finally gave in and the night now commanded the sky. The high beams threw a white beam of light out and Tom followed it carefully. John pointed ahead, "Another mile and we'll be at the border Tom, be careful, I'm sure there'll be a road block, it'll be the army or at least the police."

Tom nodded and carried on following the beams of light in front of him but as they approached the border with England there was no army, no police, not even the signs there had been a road block. The road looked just as it did all the way from the inn: deserted, clear in some places, littered with the bodies of cars and trucks in others.

John's heart sank, he had been holding on to the hope that it was confined to Scotland; that whatever this was, whatever was happening, wouldn't have affected his family but now they had passed over the border and he was in England he knew in his heart it did. He sighed and sank his head down into his chest.

Paul reached across and placed a heavy hand on John's left shoulder, squeezing it. "It'll be okay John, you'll see, they'll be fine, we're still miles from home, we've only just left Scotland."

John raised his head and smiled a little, turning to Paul he spoke softly, "But what if it isn't? what if, like everyone else, they're gone or worse they're…" He broke off and Paul could see by the moonlight a single tear roll down the big man's face.

John gulped, "What if they're like Lee?"

Paul took his hand back. He had no answers for him. He had nothing he could offer him in comfort partly because he know John was right and partly because even though it seemed certain now they had been asleep for a long time, after today he was exhausted and he simply had nothing else to give.

Outside the night had closed in and the Landrover kept its steady course towards the first town they would pass in England, Berwick. As they approached the junction that would continue them South, or into Berwick itself, Tom stopped the car. Inside the three men sat quietly; only the sound of the engine ticking over broke the silence until Tom spoke. "What now?" He turned to John, who sat in silence before turning slowly to face them both, "Just over the junction there is a garage and a supermarket. I say we head inside, see if there is anyone there and fill the car up."

"What if there isn't?" Tom asked.

"We take some food and fill the car up, Tom, same plan, just no people."

"What if there are people and they're like Lee?" Paul asked from the back.

John and Tom turned slowly to face him and then looked at each other.

"Then we take some food and fill the car up very quickly," John replied. "Either way we need food and the car needs fuel or we'll be walking and we'll be hungry!"

"It's settled then," Tom answered and engaged 1st gear. The Landrover set off over the junction and turned away from the road south and home.

Inside the garage shop the CCTV cameras recorded the Landrover turning into the forecourt and pulling up behind pump number 4. All the pumps were still occupied, some still had the nozzles in the cars, others were left lying on the ground; the fuel they had spilt long since evaporated in the hot days that had passed since the purple rain had cleared and the skies had turned a deep blue.

"What do we do, all the pumps are taken?" Tom asked.

"We move them…" John replied and gestured to Paul to help him. They slowly climbed out of the Landrover and walked to the car that was sitting on the pump they needed. As they reached it John could see that it was still open, the keys still in the ignition and the petrol cap still fastened tight.

"Looks like this guy didn't even manage to put any petrol in before he went!"

Paul opened the door of the little Fiat and sat in the driver's seat taking hold of the keys. As with the inn and on the roads, the owner's phone and wallet were laying on the passenger's seat.

"STOP!" John said quietly but firmly. "Don't start it, we'll push it."

Paul turned from his position, "Push it?"

John knelt down in the gap between the open door and white fuel pump. "What if there are more like Lee around here? They might hear the engine start."

Paul pointed over his shoulder to the ticking sound of the Landrover. "And that?"

"That's a constant sound, it may not spark any interest but an engine starting is different…just take the damn handbrake off and I'll push you in front of the garage shop."

Paul shook is head in one last point of defiance to John's logic, but in real terms it didn't matter if it was started or not, John was easily able to move the little car away from the pump and

Paul left it as he had found it, the keys in the ignition and the doors and windows closed.

Tom pulled the Discovery adjacent to the pump, but didn't switch off the engine, he climbed out and removed the fuel cap and lifted the pump from its resting place then stood.

"What are you waiting for?" asked Paul as he walked back towards him for where he had left the Fiat.

"The pump needs authorising," Tom answered.

"Come on, we'll go do that and get some stuff from the shop while we're there," John replied.

Tom watched his new friends walk towards the shop. The Landrover was warm inside; kept that way by the constant flow of warm air drawn off the engines cooling system but it wasn't out here; a cold wind from the North Sea coast seemed to blow straight through him, he looked around at the unfamiliar surroundings he found himself in street lights and the forecourt lights all seemed to be on power was still being supplied but the majority of the houses were in darkness; only the shops and the supermarket in front of them were lit up. No doubt because of the timers which would automatically turn lights on and off at set times as well as other things like the in-shop displays and the god awful music they insist on playing, the type that takes the latest hits and turns them into soft instrumental versions or worse — still gets a session singer to re-record them! Tom's attention was pulled back to the here and now by the pump clicking into life. He looked at the garage shop and he could see John smiling at him though the assistant's window. He put the fuel nozzle into the filler neck and pulled the trigger, instantly diesel started to flow filling the Landover's tank for the journey home.

After what seemed a very long time the pump clicked back and Tom knew the tank was once again full, he replaced the nozzle and the filler cap and climbed back in to his familiar and more importantly: warm driver's seat.

Paul and John walked across the deserted forecourt, walking between the abandoned cars and vans that were still waiting patiently for their fuel. Reaching the warmth and relative safety of Tom's car they climbed back in.

"Before we go," Paul started, "why don't we rest for the night, we could go into the supermarket and stay there; start off again tomorrow in the daylight."

John turned to him, "But what about getting home? what about Sam and Mickey?"

Tom placed both hands on the steering wheel and sighed, the sigh caught John's attention and he turned to face him, "Paul's right, John. I'm tired. I want to find Lynne but I won't do it falling asleep at the wheel like those poor bastards back there." He pointed back up the road they had travelled down that day.

John looked at them both, he just wanted to get home, he needed to make sure his family were okay, he needed to settle the argument that was taking place in his mind between the optimistic part that was telling him all is and will be fine and the other part, the dark side of his brain that flooded him with images and scenarios he didn't dare to acknowledge. Like some hidden monster rampaging through his mind poking at him from inside niggling away at him trying to make him conceive that his family were missing or dead or worse: they were like Lee. But he was beaten too, he was tired and the thought of another seven hours or more (*given the time it took just to get here with all the smashed cars*) made him feel worse than he thought he could and so reluctantly he agreed.

"Okay, just for tonight but we can't leave the car out the front." He turned back to face Tom, "Drop me and Paul off at the entrance then drive round the back to the goods in doors, we'll pull them open and you can drive it there for tonight. Plus we can put more supplies in it while it's in there."

Paul leaned forward, "Isn't that stealing?"

John turned to look at him with an expression of irritation on his face, "Leave them your fuckin' credit card if you're worried!"

Tom sniggered and started for the supermarket.

As they approached it the supermarket looked no different than it would normally; cars parked neatly in the designated parking places waiting for their owners to return and fill the boot with bags of food or whatever it was they had gone there to buy, but it was as they drew closer they started to notice the familiar pattern: phones left on the ground laying uselessly next to more wallets, purses and hand bags, carrier bags of spilt food lay next to some cars whose tailgates and boot lids still waited in the open position. Some cars had the doors open as well, no doubt whatever this was had happened just as the owners were getting in or getting out.

"Why did they have time to drop their phones and bags but not shut the door or lock the car?" thought Tom, but he didn't ask it out loud, John had enough on his mind and if he hadn't noticed this Tom wasn't about to bring it to his attention and anyway Tom was fighting his own mind monsters and like John's showed him pictures of Sam and Mickey, Tom's showed him what had happened to Lynne!

Tom weaved slowly and purposefully towards the entrance bouncing the abandoned shopping trolleys off the large front bumpers every time he simply ran out of manoeuvring room. Even at this slow speed one knock from the Landrover sent them scurrying across the car park until they turned over or hit something else; usually a parked car.

"Tom, try not to hit every damn trolley, it makes a hell of a noise," Paul said whispering through his clenched teeth.

"Sorry, but there just isn't room and unless you want to get out and move them…" Tom started to argue back to stand his ground. He didn't take kindly to having his driving criticised, in fact Lynne used to say that the only reason he bought such a big car was because whilst he was driving it he felt on equal terms with the much larger men he would eventually have to walk amongst. 'Little man syndrome', she would say to him. But John interrupted both of them, pointing straight ahead, "Just pull up there Tom, then drive round the back." John's tone was sharp and to the point, but more than that — it was focused and Tom knew trying to pick up on Paul's point now would be futile and pointless. He did as he was instructed and stopped close to the main doors. John and Paul climbed out and then watched as the Landrover headed off and rounded the corner following the large 'Goods in' sign.

Inside it was deserted, shopping trolleys full and half full and even empty were scattered around the store; the same as outside, left exactly where they had been abandoned by the shoppers that had been using them. Some of them next to the fruit and vegetables which had now started to turn bad, others at the news stand. Magazines and papers left strewn on the floor; newspapers displayed headlines from what to John and Paul now seemed a life time ago. And again phones and bags left behind with everything else.

"Do you think its safe in here?" Paul asked.

"Honestly, I don't know, but if we lock it up it'll be safe enough and we'll have all the food and drink we need...and the power's still on."

Paul turned slowly on the spot. A look of slight confusion came across his face.

"How do we lock it up? We don't have keys for the front doors and finding them in this place could take forever."

John walked towards the side of the large glass doors that welcomed the paying customers in and ushered the paid customers out. "

No we don't have the keys for the doors but the keys for steel shutters outside are still in the control box, at least we can drop them."

He turned the key in the little metal grey box to the picture that undoubtedly meant *'down'* and instantly the steel shutters started the journey down until with a rattle they sealed the entrance from the outside. As John stepped back away from the control box and out of range of the senses that would open the large glass doors they too closed behind him.

The two men walked past the customer service desk, news stands and rotting vegetable trays towards the back of the store.

"Through here," John pointed to the staffing area next to the fish counter; the smell of the rotting fish stuck in the back of their throats as they passed by it, pushing through the heavy plastic see through doors into the warehouse behind the store; the area the paying public never gets to see.

They passed what seemed to be endless lines of un-opened goods from all areas of the store: large screen TVs, light bulbs, toilet paper, toasters and candles; in fact everything you would find in a large self-contained supermarket that wants to ensure that whatever it is you need no matter what time of day it is or even what day it is you only need to shop here and nowhere else.

They found the control for the loading doors and John pushed the green button that said 'Open'. The door juddered and started moving up, as it lifted, the headlamp beams of the Landrover shone in to the partly-lit warehouse. Once John was happy the door was high enough he hit the red 'Stop' button and the door shuddered to a halt. Paul waved his arm at Tom and he drove the Landrover in. The door started its descent down behind the car and just as Tom stopped the car the door stopped, now fully closed. Tom extinguished the lights and turned the engine off, the clacking sound of the diesel engine that had accompanied them since leaving the inn now fell silent, and the warehouse too fell into an uneasy silence. Tom climbed out and walked round towards John and Paul.

They made their way through the store collecting the things they felt they would need, things like: batteries, torches, pens, maps and of course food and water; not the things they had always assumed they would take should they have ever found themselves in an empty supermarket with everyone else gone. Things like large LED TVs, 3D Blueray players, ipods, the latest digital cameras and all the other *'boys' toys'* a store like this would sell. It seemed that now the world had changed. These things no longer had any place in it, and anyway why watch a sci-fi or horror movie when they were becoming more convinced that they were now in one.

With the Landrover packed up they made their way to the staff room and settled in for the night with the food and treats they had liberated from the shelves in the store, for now the electricity was still on and with the door shut tight and barricaded from the inside just in case someone like Lee was lurking around the store or had found a way in through a door they had missed. They made themselves as comfortable as they could and tried to let their minds catch up on all that had happened since they had woken up earlier that day. Placing the empty wrappers in the bin that had the usual corporate sign placed perfectly above it by some over-enthusiastic assistant manager: *'Please place all your rubbish in the bin provided and leave the area clean for your colleagues'*.

John pointed to the notice board on the wall.

"Look at all this, all these spreadsheets and league tables in sales and customer complaints, all this really is just crap, isn't it? I mean, who cares?"

He pointed to the name at the top of the table.

"That James has sold more TVs than Rob or that Janice has sold more than Andrew D, really? who fucking cares?"

Paul agreed with him, "I know, imagine all the time and effort not to mention the paper that's put to use just to measure how many people have walked through the doors of the store."

"Footfall," Tom interrupted him.

"What?"

"It's called footfall, that's how they measure how many people have come through the doors, then they chart what times most people come in and what they buy, that way they can plan their part-time staff and stocking levels more accurately."

"How the hell do you know that?" asked Paul.

"Because I'm in retail. I'm a consultant. I go round and tell stores like this one how to run leaner and how to make more profit…that's what I do."

A silence fell over the staff room before Tom continued, but not after he had sighed and looked around the room slowly as if he was desperate to be back doing what he does, standing in meeting rooms with his laptop and portable projector showing managers how he can maximise their stores' profits and cash flows and drive the business forward in a dynamic and *out of the box* way!

"But you're right, of course, Paul, if everybody has gone, if we're all that's left then all the tables, records, charts, invoices, accounts and reports are all just meaningless pieces of paper or digital files on a hard drive somewhere that's probably never going to be accessed again."

John turned to face him, "So you think this is it? You think we are all that's left?"

"I don't know, John. I mean, shit! I hope not. I hope that maybe a little further South we find the line you thought might have been at the Scottish border, maybe they had to drop back; maybe they'll be just over the next hill."

"But what if they're not?" Paul interrupted Tom's attempt at optimism.

"What if we have somehow witnessed and missed the end of humanity? I mean, all those people in the inn, all those cars crashed and abandoned and here on the petrol forecourt and in the shop. If people were being evacuated for their own good and it was quick, why leave all the IDs behind? and why leave all the phones? What if families were separated, how do they get in touch with each other if their IDs and phones were left behind?"

John sat upright, his face changed. "Do we know if the networks are still up? I mean, we haven't tried; our batteries were dead so we couldn't."

The three of them turned their attention to the little phone that sat on the kitchen worktop behind them where the microwave oven and kettle sat with just enough room for staff to make a cup of tea or coffee and nuke a TV dinner; that they would rush down in a hurry before they were called back to the shop floor. The little phone sat on the counter, still plugged in and still charging. Tom was the first to stand up, he looked at John and Paul as he made his way slowly round the back of his chair towards the phone. Picking it up and sliding the cover open, the screen came to life, holding it in his hand he looked back again towards John and pressed the dial button. Slowly Tom raised the phone towards his ear and as he pressed it against it he could hear nothing but the dead sounding no service tone, even if their batteries had been charged their phones now were nothing but pieces of plastic and circuit boards. John could tell the line was dead, he could tell by the expression of dismay on Tom's face, the look of hope that he had worn as he picked the phone up had long gone and as Tom turned and carefully placed the phone back down Paul spoke.

"So that's it then, we are on our own."

John was the first to speak and he spoke quietly, almost whispering, his head bowed low and his hands clasped together.

"I hope not, because that would mean Sam and Mickey have gone." He turned his head, to look at Paul.

John's eyes were raw and red but not for the same reason Lee's had been. Paul's words about them being the last ones had driven into John's heart. The thought that he would never see Sam and Mickey was becoming almost unbearable, like a weight on his chest; a crushing nauseating weight, and no matter how hard he tried and which ever way he reasoned with it, or whichever scenario he came up with about how they must have escaped, or been missed; as he was, he could not get rid of it, that feeling, that thought that something terrible had happened to them. Tears ran down his face as he continued in his whisper, "Where do you suppose everybody is? Did the government do this; did we evacuate everybody from the UK? Do you think they're safe, Paul?"

Paul had no answer, how could he have? he had no idea what had happened, he knew the same as John and Tom, but he answered his friend and he replied in the same soft whispering tones that John had used, partly because he felt it would be soothing but mostly because he was simply exhausted and at this point he couldn't have shouted if his life did depend on it.

"Honestly, John, I don't know but I do know Sam and I do know she would never ever let anything happen to Mickey wherever they are and whoever it is that has evacuated everybody. I know she's taking good care of him."

John smiled and wiped away the last of the tears that ran down his face.

Paul continued, "Now I think we should sleep, and tomorrow we'll be home and then you'll see."

"See what?" Tom interrupted.

"You'll see that everybody is safe."

Tom smiled and turned over in his temporary bed for the night. "We'll see," he said, as he pulled the camping cover he had borrowed from the store over his head. One by one the three men fell into a deep dreamless sleep.

The following day started early for them with the sounding of an alarm. Tom woke first pulling the blankets down from over his face and twisting out of the chair he'd been curled up most of the night. Slowly his world came into focus and then the sound of the alarm became the prominent thing in his mind. It wasn't the type of alarm to warn you like the shrill of a fire alarm or the panicking sound of the burglar alarm; it was a soft *'Please wake up, it's time to get up, come on, please get up'* alarm and Tom realised very quickly it was coming from the little phone he had tried the previous night. Neither Tom, John or Paul wore watches. Like a lot of people they thought watches were all but redundant with the new generation of smart phones; they were the watches now and the diaries and alarms and much more. He climbed out of his chair and walked very stiffly around where the phone chimed and pressed the exit button which was now brightly lit instantly. The phone fell silent once again and Tom realised that the alarm would have been set by the owner and was no doubt set at this time to get them out of their bed and then he followed that thought up... how many phones and alarm clocks were going off now around the country or even the world to empty beds? and what about other automatic things like fridge freezers and central heating timers? how many homes were right now warming themselves up for their occupants to get up to warm rooms and warm water to shower in only for there to be nobody!

Tom's attention snapped back just as John and Paul climbed from their makeshift bunks. Paul looked exhausted and John didn't seem to be much better but he was ready to go; he wanted to waste no time, he wanted to get home but first they had to eat and wash and to do that they used the staff canteen and showers. John was getting dressed when Tom came in. "You better come see this." Pulling his shirt on he followed Tom out and back into the store towards the large front glass windows. They walked down isle 7 through the cereals and biscuits, all neatly stacked and displayed and towards the checkouts where Paul was crouched behind checkout stand 6 looking intently out of the front of the store towards the car park.

"What it is?" asked John.

Tom gestured for him to join Paul and himself crouching down.

"Look!" was the only reply Paul made and once John saw what he was watching it was all he needed. Outside stumbling between two parked cars was a man dressed in a mechanic's blue oil-stained overall. His face was dirty, covered in oil and grime from his working day. The three men watched as he fell into the side of the Audi which had been carefully parked by its owner who no doubt had had every intention of returning to it and filling the boot with the groceries they needed. He stumbled into the driver's door mirror and instantly flew into a rage; his face screwed up with anger, his eyes looked like Lee's just before he had flown at Tom. Raising his right hand he let out an incomprehensible scream and brought his hand down on the mirror which gave way instantly; snapping off, now being held onto the car only by the wires that supplied the electric motor and heating element. He raised his hand again and they could see that it wasn't only the car that had suffered from the impact, blood ran freely from his hand, it was obvious that the car had managed to inflict some damage of its own but as he brought his hand back down again severing the wires and sending the mirror crashing to the ground it was also very obvious to them that he had no idea he was bleeding so badly and it dawned on them that he didn't even know he had been injured! Satisfied with the retribution he had carried out on the Audi he once again staggered between it and the Peugeot parked next to it. His movements were awkward and stiff and as with Lee, his arms flayed around as he grunted and ticked, his skin had the same colour as Lee's *(under the oil and grease that covered him)* and his eyes were the same blood shot mad-looking eyes, as if all humanity had been taken from them. His head moved from side to side looking around the car park and as he came from between the two cars he stood twitching, carefully scouting his surroundings, blood still dripped from his hand and now he was still, it started to pool on the black tarmac. He looked directly into the shop and Tom thought at him, he grimaced and pulled back, "Shit! he's seen us."

"No, he hasn't," John assured him, "he's just looking at the shop, he can't see us behind here but I've seen enough, let's get to the Landrover and head out."

Paul nodded. The three men slowly and very carefully backed away from the checkout stand and headed back down the cereal isle and through the back of the shop towards the waiting car. Tom climbed into his driving seat and turned the engine over, almost instantly the diesel engine fired up and ticked over while John pushed the open button for the large metal *up'n'over* door. As the door started to raise Tom backed the Landrover out of the warehouse, once it was clear John pushed the close button and joined his two friends in the car. As they set off back towards the road South that would take them home, Paul watched as the metal door slammed shut sealing the supermarket off from the outside. As Tom rounded the corner of the store and headed back into the main car park he hit the brakes and the two-tonne Discovery rocked to an abrupt halt. "Shit!" was the only word that he could think to speak and John could see why. Directly ahead with his back towards them was the mechanic standing in the middle of the lane that would take them clear and back on to the road. At the sound of the engine he started to turn jerking his body in lunging deliberate movements, his gaze fixed directly on them and his mad soulless

75

eyes seemed to fix on all three of them at the same time.

"What do I do?" Tom asked nervously.

John turned to face him and he could see the sheer panic and terror on his face. His hands gripped the steering wheel very tightly, so tightly in fact that his knuckles had already turned white.

"What do you mean what do you do? Put your foot down and drive past him!" John's tone was one of weight, he meant what he had said; this wasn't a suggestion — this was a command and it did the trick. Tom planted his foot hard on the accelerator and the Landrover raised its nose and charged head on at the man in front of them. As they got closer he started the same scream he had let out when he had smashed the door mirror off, "Oh, shit, shit, shit!" Tom repeated to himself as he headed for him. His foot wanted to back off the pedal and hit the brake but his mind kept over-riding it; remembering the feeling of imminent attack and no doubt death when Lee had attacked him was enough for him to keep going, but it was going against all his years of driving; he had always had the natural impulse to stop or at least slow to avoid obstacles in the road but he was sure — as sure as he could be — that this obstacle would be quiet happy to kill him and his friends if it had the chance and so Tom kept his foot flat to the floor, at the last second he flinched the steering wheel to the right the front driver's side of Landrover; hit the rear bumper of the Nissan Micra that was parked opposite to where the man stood, the force tore off the Nissan's bumper and smashed the car into the lamp post next to it. The passenger's side of the Landrover hit the mechanic. He was spun around by the impact and sent reeling into the parked cars. John watched as he crashed into the back of a small car, he couldn't tell what type it was; to him they all looked pretty much the same, but the force of the impact sent him up and over the boot lid smashing into the rear window of the car. The hand that still bled smashed through the glass sending him half-way into the back of it but by now Tom had navigated his way round the one-way system, put in place by the supermarket to keep the traffic flowing through, and he was on the main road heading back towards the roundabout which would take them onto the road home and hopefully to Lynne, Sam, and Mickey.

Chapter Four
The Tank

John walked out of the back door of his house; he could see Sam sitting in the large swing chair they had picked out together and Mickey sat on his *Jack Blanky* with his toys scattered around him; amongst them his two favourite toys: the *Jet Liner* John had once brought him back while he had been working in America and his T Rex. The sun shone down and the air felt warm and sweet. Sam smiled at him as he walked towards her, even his steps felt effortless as if he was floating his way to her, his bare feet felt the warmth of the short green grass and as he sat beside her, her soft blonde hair gleamed in the strong light and the laughs of Mickey filled his heart with a warmth that simply could not be described. It was in fact the perfect day with the perfect weather and they sat in the back garden of their perfect home. The sky was the deepest blue with no clouds the sun shone a brilliant yellow and it felt warm and nurturing; he could look into it without any pain to his eyes; with no need to squint or to hold his hands in front of him. It was just right, everything was just right, and he could hear the bird song — it was almost as if they were serenading them both, singing to them in this absolute picture of paradise. Relaxing back into her shoulder he watched Mickey play, his large blue eyes filled with the wonder and imagination that is there for just the briefest of moments as a child before we grow up and see the world around us for what it is. A feeling of absolute well-being filled John completely. She softly swept her hand across his forehead, he reached across to take hold of it as he looked up into her deep blue eyes. "I love you," he said, a smile with the warmth of the sun spread across her face. "I know, sweetheart and I love you too, but now you have to go, we've gone and now you have to." The feeling of absolute well-being now washed away and confusion started to tumble down over him.

"What?"

"It's time to go," Sam continued.

""He's gone, look," she pointed to Mickey's Jack Blanky.

John sat up away from her and looked to where his son had been playing, but he was gone, only the blanket remained with a few toys scattered around it.

"Where is he?"

Sam smiled again, but this time it wasn't the warm loving smile it was smile of defeat and sadness. Her face now looked pale and gloomy and her eyes had lost the gleam and light that was there only a short time ago. The sky too now became grey and leaden, thunder rumbled in the distance.

"I love you, John but now I have to go."

"No... Sam, no!"

John cried out but she was gone and now he sat alone, both of them had vanished, disappeared from sight, almost as if they had evaporated before him.

Suddenly the large swing chair juddered violently and John was pushed forward out of it. He put his hands out to protect himself from the inevitable impact of the ground but found himself with his hands pressed hard against the dashboard of the Landrover. Confused and dazed he turned to see Tom staring ahead.

"What do you suppose that's doing there?" he said bewildered.

John turned to look at Paul who sat half-smiling at him,

"You having a bad dream?"

The feeling of realisation came on him, he had been dreaming. He'd been back in his garden with his family but now he was back in reality and right now he wished with all his heart they could be the other way round.

Paul pointed forward, "That's why we had to stop."

John turned back to look out of the front window and directly ahead of them parked across the road sat a tank, its massive gun pointing directly at them and under its huge metal tracks was a crushed car.

"Jesus!" was the only response John could

manage to the sudden change from the serenity of his garden to facing down the immense gun of the tank.

"Do you think there's anybody in it?" Tom asked.

"I'm not sure I want to know," Paul replied, and continued, "can't we get around it?"

"I don't know, it's completely blocking the road and we don't know what's on the other side of it."

"Tom's right, we need to get out and look, Paul."

John sounded as sure as he always did, and that look of certainty that Paul often found comfort in when working in the harsh conditions they did was back. The dream that John had wished was real; was long gone and no doubt would be forgotten soon enough like all dreams are, for now his concentration was focused on the huge leviathan that blocked their way south and home.

They climbed out of the Landrover and started to walk slowly over to the tank. Its massive size became ever more intimidating as they approached it. John reached up and placed his right hand on the end of the gun.

"What is it?" asked Paul.

"It's a Challenger 2, it's the main battle tank for the British Army," he replied.

Tom walked up along side them and touched the gun with John, hesitantly at first then placing the flat of his hand against the cold steel.

"That might be what it is John, but like I said, why is it here, parked across the road?"

John pulled his hand down and turned to him, "I have no idea Tom, but then I have no idea of what's going on generally. I mean, do you?"

He walked away from them leaving Tom standing with his hand still pressed against the gun and headed for the front of the hull where he knew the driver's view port would be.

Tom pulled his hand down and looked down the hull of the tank. The eight massive wheels that supported the large tracks sat almost flatly against the black Tarmac, it looked to him as if it had grown there right out of the ground, it looked solid and indestructible — only the remains of the crushed car under it forced the wheels out of their perfect alignment with the road.

"I wonder how long it's been here," Paul asked.

"It can't have been long, why?"

Tom turned to Paul and pointed at the car under the tank, "Because that blood is fresh!"

Paul followed Tom's finger and from the passenger's side of the crushed car he could see a hand and from under that they could see that a steady stream of blood had ran, and even though the blood had now stopped making its escape from whoever the unfortunate soul was, it hadn't yet dried and was in the sticky congealing stage. Paul raised his hand to his mouth and fought with the impulse to empty his stomach, "What do you suppose happened here Tom?"

John had reached the main hull of the tank and started the climb onto it, as he did a voice called out: "Back away from the tank, or we will open fire, we are authorised to use live rounds." John stopped immediately, half on and half off the tank; he froze as if playing a life and death version of statues, slowly he pulled the hand and foot he had on the hull off and backed away a few feet, a cold chill ran down him. "Who are you, why are you here?" John waited for the reply, he seemed to wait a life time, even standing next to this thing was intimidating now he knew someone was inside, it made him feel relieved and terrified at the same time, the thought of someone with all that's happened commanding all the power it had made him feel vulnerable, and that wasn't something he enjoyed.

Paul and Tom came around the gun to join him, the three men now stood in front of it but there was still no answer. John tried again, "Do you know what's happening here? Do you know anything about this?" He shouted as loud as he could straining his voice. "We just want to get home, to see our families." Still silence. John moved again towards the hull but

83

Tom grabbed his arm.

"John, you can't do anything with this, we'll find another way round we'll go through Jedburgh, join up with the A1 further down."

He turned to Tom, angry and frustrated, a look of both filled his face and Tom instantly let go of his arm backing away slightly, even Paul hadn't seen his friend like that.

"That means doubling back heading through the National Park, it'll add hours onto the journey, and we're not doing that, they can move this fucking thing or I will!" He turned away from Tom and as he did they heard the metallic clank of locks detaching.

Suddenly the upper hatch on the turret opened and a man wearing a British Army uniform emerged from it. Paul raised his hands to protect his eyes from the harsh sunlight of the afternoon, the silhouetted figure climbed further out of the hatch until he stood up right on the tank before making his way down and climbing off the hull. He walked towards John and held out an open hand

"Hello, I'm Alec, I'm the tank commander." He took hold of John's hand and shook it with the authority and strength John might have expected from someone who was in charge of something like this.

"I'm John." He turned and pointed to his travelling companions, "This is Paul and Tom."

"Nice to meet you." Alec gestured towards

them and then placed a tentative hand around John's back pulling round a little and away from them.

"We saw you coming over to us, but we had to be sure you were okay. We can't move, we've busted a track on the other side so we're stuck fast I'm afraid but you should be able to get around us in your Landrover."

John pulled away from his guiding hand. "What do you mean you had to make sure we were alright?"

Alec stood for a while looking puzzled at John. A small smile spread across his face as if he were expecting John to suddenly admit to knowing what he was referring to but John didn't and Alec soon pulled the smile back.

"You know the rejects?"

"Rejects?" John still confused repeated the name back to Alec, but by this time seeing the expression of bewilderment on his face, Tom and Paul come over and joined in the conversation.

"What are you talking about, rejects?"

Alec looked uncomfortable. He shifted around on the spot, he reminded John of a child that had suddenly been caught out in a lie and had no where else to go with it, knowing that now they had to tell the truth.

"The rain, that rain that came down, you must have seen it." Alec began but John cut across him, "Seen it, we drove right through it and woke up three weeks later!" "Everybody did, except there"...Alec was cut off, their attention caught by a howl and another then another.

"Shit, with me," Alec shouted at them as he turned and headed back for the tank.

"What?" Tom shouted after him but Alec was already on the hull.

"Either get in here with me or get back to your car and hope it'll keep them out!"

"Keep what out?" asked Paul.

"Whatever is coming through those trees!"

Suddenly the howls started again. Alec now at the hatch shouted at the three stationary men again, "Last chance!"

He waved his arm at them gesturing them to get onto the tank and John didn't wait for another invitation and the latest howl was enough for Paul and Tom to follow.

Alec gestured them down into the tank, John was the first inside followed by Paul. Tom missed the first step down. "Move it!" Alec commanded as the howls came again. Tom dropped inside and Alec was finally able to drop down and seal the hatch behind him. As John navigated his way round the cramped interior he saw another man sitting in what he assumed to be the driver's seat. He moved over to him and shook his hand. "I'm John, this is Paul and Tom." The driver smiled at all three of them. "Private Duncan, Sir, I'm the driver, well at least I was before this."

John could tell that Duncan knew something; he must have some idea of what was going on and what had spooked Alec so much.

Inside the tank it was almost silent, only the on board sights and cameras allowed them to see outside. Duncan had firmly closed his driver's hatch and had engaged the optical view finder and even though the tank was now stranded; the tracks ripped off by the very car they had crushed and centre reservation barriers, he still left it firmly closed.

John turned away from Duncan and faced Alec head on knowing that he had nowhere now to move to or go to. Until they knew what was going on and what that was out there none of them were going anywhere.

The interior was cramped and dim, no sunlight penetrated in now that it was sealed, only the small interior lights and glow of the monitors illuminated the dark small steel box they now found themselves in. The air felt thick and used, heat from the on board computers had nowhere to go and the smell of sweat lingered in every corner.

"Now, tell me what these rejects are, what that is out there." Alec still looked uncomfortable, as if he shouldn't be sharing this with a civilian or worse still — he hadn't expected to see a civilian ever again. He removed his cap and rubbed his hands through his short blonde hair and sat back into his commander's seat. The three men looked intensely at him. Both John and Paul knew this could explain what had happened to their friend Lee back at the inn.

"We don't know exactly what it is," Alec started, "we had very little warning, what with Seti closing down a few weeks ago, some of them thought that's what they had been waiting for,"…John cut him off, "What? Who had been waiting for? and Seti, what's that?

Alec shifted in his seat but as he started to answer Tom interrupted him, "It stands for the *Search for Extra Terrestrial Intelligence,* that's right isn't it, Alec?"

Alec looked across the three of them and nodded, "It stopped looking in April this year due to budget cuts, some think once that happened they took their chance."

John stopped him again raising his hand up; not like a child would wanting to get the teacher's attention but as he did with Lee; like a police officer stopping a car, "You keep saying *they* took their chance, who are *they?"*

"We don't know exactly. It all happened too fast, we had no time to respond. One minute everything was normal but by the time we knew something was happening most of our response forces were asleep: pilots, commanders, captains on ships — all asleep. Christ, even the Prime Minister and Secretary of Defence, who issue the orders for us to engage, were gone. We estimate 92% of our defence and fighting force were out of action and the planes that were airborne fell out of the skies with the pilots fast asleep in the cockpit. As for the rest of the soldiers and sailors; only people like us in sealed environments didn't succumb to it, but we had no chain of command, no-one to guide us to where we needed to be, we simply didn't know what was happening so we fell back to our standard strategy should this happen."

"And what's that?" asked Paul.

"We split up, made ourselves harder for the enemy to find and went on *seek and destroy,* since then I've heard nothing from anybody."

Alec stopped and took a deep breath, he released it slowly, sighing as he did, and then looked over at Duncan and continued, "The last orders we had were to take a scientist down to Whitehall. These tanks have a sealed environment in case of biological warfare, that's why we weren't affected, no air got in. No air, no rain but we grounded here yesterday on the car and crash barrier. I sent the gunner and the loader on with him in another car that was abandoned,..." Tom interrupted him, "A scientist, so they knew something was going to happen over here?"

Alec looked between the three of them with a puzzled expression. "Over here?"

"I meant you know here, we thought at first it was just Scotland, we thought we would find a line at the English border but when we didn't we assumed it must be further South."

Alec's expression of puzzlement changed to a smile, it was a look that John knew meant *You poor dumb bastards* and then he spoke, "The Scottish border? this is worldwide, this is everywhere, every country, every part of the Earth, and all at the same time. The scientist told us they had an idea, an inclining that something was about to happen but they were caught completely by surprise. By the time the rain started the best we could do was dive our submarines and try to use sealed vehicles like this to take the people who could stop it to where they needed to be."

"Submarines?" Paul asked.

"They're still submerged, waiting for commands that will never come to."

John fell back in his seat. A feeling of absolute acceptance started to wash over him and the monster in his mind started to draw pictures again of his life without Sam and Mickey, but he had to push it back, take control of it again, he pushed himself forward leaning in close to Alec. "But you still haven't told us what you meant by seeing if we were okay and what you were so scared of out there."

Alec backed away from John, he may have been a tank commander but John was still a good five inches taller and what looked like two or three stone heavier and in this confined space that was enough.

"We know some people didn't disappear, we don't know why yet but we have found stragglers like you." He paused... "How come you're here?"

"The car we were travelling in crashed, it was covered by shrubs and bushes, hidden from the road."

John pointed to Tom, "And I found him stuck between a door and a wall in the toilets, I didn't see him when I walked in." Alec nodded, "That could explain it,..." John interrupted him again, "You were telling us about the rain." Alec continued, "for some reason — and we don't know why — the rain seems to..." he paused and shifted around looking more and more uneasy, "it seems to affect some people and animals, they lose all control; they become enraged and violent but more than that they lose all reasoning powers; all communication skills seem to go and they attack anybody or anything they see."

"The mechanic and the Audi!" Tom said.

"What?"

Tom looked at Alec and shook his head, "Back down the road we watched one, he bumped into and Audi and smashed the mirror off."

Alec nodded, "Like I said, extremely violent with no ability it seems to communicate."

"But you called them rejects?" John pressed him.

"Not me, the scientist. That's what he called them, he said their bodies had rejected whatever process the rain did to them, so...rejects."

"My friend is back there, he became like you described. I've known him for years and he's a fucking REJECT!" Paul's face was red with anger and temper, John turned to him, "He was my friend too and it wasn't Alec that coined the phrase...remember?"

Paul nodded. His expression had already started to calm.

"So what was howling?" Tom asked.

All of them had forgotten about the noise that had forced them into the tank to take refuge. They couldn't hear it anymore, inside the tank was silent to what was going on outside.

"Dogs," Alec replied.

"Dogs? What kind of dogs howl like that?"

"As I said, the rain affects animals the same as people, except no animals seemed to have disappeared, only people."

Tom's face turned white, a look of dismay washed over it. "You're telling us that there are animals out there like his friend: berserk, mad and violent?"

Alec nodded and pointed to one of the multiple screens that decorated the walls of the tank. The three men moved round to view and there outside gnarling and chewing at the hand that stuck out of the crushed car were two dogs and as with Lee and the mechanic there was something very obviously wrong with them. Their coats had clumps of fur missing, dried blood stains surrounded the ears of both dogs, the movements were hard and jagged and through the green glare of the camera's all light lens's they could see clearly their eyes were bulging and blood shot. Tom spoke first as they watched but it was soft, almost a whisper. Partly, John thought because he was saddened by yet something else that had to be a dream but wasn't but he also thought because Tom was worried they would hear him even though they were safe for now.

"So what happened to him?" He pointed down at the screen, "the person in the car?"

Alec's gaze didn't turn away from the screen, he answered him without so much a hesitation. "He was one of them, we spotted him as we came down the road, he must have heard us because he turned and stood his ground."

"So, you just ran him down?" John asked.

"We were told to, we were told not to leave them, to kill on site — no questions, in case someone like...well, like you came along. Unfortunately Duncan didn't see the crash barrier, we snagged on it and tore that track off." John smiled and laughed a little, "So here we are trapped inside a tin can that can't move and can't fire."

"Fire?" remarked Alec.

"You said you sent the gunner and loader away with the scientist."

"Yes I did and I did it because there is nothing to fire at. What? you think we'd use the main gun on those dogs?"

John's smile slid away, "I have no idea. All I can see is that we're stuck here until they go away."

It won't be long," Duncan said.

"And how do you know that?" Tom replied.

"Because it's dark in a few hours, the reje........." he stopped half-way through, mindful of Paul's remark at the term Alec had used, and then he continued..."these things, the ones that turned, they only come out in the day; we've never seen one in the dark…ever!"

"This scientist, what car did they leave in?" Tom asked Alec.

"It was a blue Rover 75, W plate, why?"

"Just in case we see them."

An uneasy quiet fell about the tank. John, Paul and Tom still didn't have all the information they needed to neatly piece together what had happened to them and everyone else they'd either seen or more worryingly, not seen, and whilst Alec had told them what he knew *(or at least he said he knew)*, it still didn't explain everything.

It was late afternoon by the time they had settled down as best they could inside the tank.

With the new information that these *Rejects* *(although it still galled them, Paul especially, to call them this)* seemed to only appear in the day; they had decided to travel at night, and as that was in only a few hours time, now it was time to sleep.

But as John rested he knew that all around the world everywhere was deserted homes, offices, businesses, all sitting empty. Universities, schools, colleges now empty. The classrooms that were once the centres of learning for the next great leaders or artists are now nothing more than vacant rooms that would soon become derelict and ruined with the passage of time. Villages, settlements and towns in the furthest reaches of human civilisation were deserted and empty. Hospitals, too, empty corridors and wards. Everything we took for granted, everything that we had built would now be consigned to history, not human history because there is simply not enough people now to preserve it, but the history of the Earth and like 99% of all the animals and species that have ever lived on this planet: our time had come.

Chapter Five
Dr Andrew Richards

As night fell, John, Paul and Tom left the tank behind. With Tom at the wheel of the Landrover they carefully negotiated their way around it and started the journey South. The high beams illuminated the road in patches of brilliant white light leaving everywhere else in a near perfect blackness, only the light of the full moon gave any peripheral light.

As the A1 turned from a single carriageway into the duel carriageway for the last time, North of Newcastle, Tom brought the Landrover to gentle stop. As it slowed the only sound was the squeak of its brakes and the continual clattering of the diesel engine, a sound that the three of them had become used to and that even offered some comfort, because they knew that this sound meant they were safe and on their way home, but for now they sat motionless; the large circular pockets of light now lit up yet another scene of carnage: smashed pieces of metal that had once been cars, trucks and buses littered both the North and South carriageways, they had smashed over onto the central barriers and up the embankments that lined either side of the four lanes.

Tom spoke first. "There's no way round this

one."

John sighed and rubbed his eyes, shaking his head, he didn't want to say what he was about to because it meant one thing, it meant ditching the Landrover and walking but he knew Tom was right, the road was completely blocked they simply had no choice.

"No there isn't Tom, we're going to be walking from here."

"Can't we turn around and find another way down?" Paul asked.

"Not really, even if we did go back over, there's nothing to say the other roads wouldn't be blocked and of course they're single roads as well. Anyway, if we walk through this we may find a car we can use further down."

"Looks like we're on foot then," Tom said.

John turned to face them both, pointing at Tom first and then Paul, "Tom, leave the lights on so we can see our way for some distance. Paul, you grab the bag of food and water behind you."

The three men climbed out and started to walk towards the smashed and tangled bits of metal that were once the owners' pride and joy.

Paul stopped and pointed over to his right, "John, what car did Alec say the scientist was in?"

"He said it was a blue Rover 75, why?"

"What plate?"

"'W' I think, why?"

"It's over there!"

John looked to where Paul was pointing and there sat the Rover.

"C'mon, let's go have a look."

Paul and Tom followed John over to the car, but as with their car it was empty, there were no signs of whoever had been in it, the doors and windows were closed and the keys still hung from the ignition.

"Shit! I thought we might have found something, anything to help us catch up."

"Why do you want to catch up?" Tom asked.

John turned away from the Rover and towards him, "Because this scientist can fill in the blanks, he maybe able to tell us what Alec couldn't."

"Or wouldn't!" Paul said.

John turned to him and nodded, "Or wouldn't! Come on let's keep going, we need to cover as much ground as we can while it's dark."

Glass cracked and broke beneath their feet as the lights from the abandoned Landrover cast eerie shadows around them. The light that did penetrate the interiors only amplified the feelings of apprehension and fear that gripped them, as with the cars they had left behind in Scotland, pools of dried blood stained them and the road next to them, and as with Scotland there were no bodies but there were phones littered everywhere; they stood on some of them, others laid on the seats of the cars, others in the holders the owners had had fitted and where there were phones there were wallets and purses and I.Ds.

What if Alec had been wrong? What if the rejects did come out at night and they just hadn't seen them? Out here in the dark with only the moonlight and the ever-decreasing light of the Landrover to guide them, they would be defenceless.

"I watched a programme on this once;" Paul said as they negotiated their way through:

"On what?" replied John.

"All this, what would happen if overnight people disappeared off the planet?"

"And what did it say?" Tom asked.

"It said that eventually nature would take the planet back, and that even the most substantial of structures would crumble because no one would be around to maintain them. Birds and cats would take over office blocks and dogs would return to pack hunting, not pedigree dogs though they said they wouldn't survive."

"Years of inbreeding," Tom added.

"It all said that once our bridges, tunnels and everything else we'd built or made crumbled there would be no signs at all of human existence."

"What about space?" Tom asked.

"Space?"

"Yeah, satellites and the space station."

"It said they would eventually fall back to Earth, finally giving in to Earth's gravitational pull, or something like that. I'm telling you, it said eventually it would be as if we had never existed at all!"

Tom didn't ask anymore questions. What Paul had just said had sent a numbing trail of dread through to his core.

"What about power, you know electricity and gas? What did it say about them?" John asked.

"It said that the power stations would keep generating power, but because no-one would be demanding it eventually they would shutdown; something to do with safety procedures to stop them from blowing up."

John turned to face him while he squeezed between the wreckage of two small cars that had no doubt hit each other at motorway speeds; judging by the way they were now almost one car, "Did it say how long they would last?"

"I think it said no more than four weeks, depending on the type of station and the area it was in; so I guess some have already gone off line and the rest will soon."

John nodded, "Thought so!"

"It's the zoos that worry me," Tom said from behind them.

"Zoos?" replied Paul.

"Yeah, imagine with no power to the electric fences and no-one to maintain them, what's to stop things like lions and tigers escaping? I mean, they're bad enough, but if the rain affected them and turned them into...you know... a reject."

John and Paul said nothing as they pushed on through what seemed to be endless smashed cars.

Eventually they started to clear the wreckage. The lights of the Landrover had long since disappeared behind them and Tom knew he would never see his car and the last thing he had that was a physical connection to Lynne again.

As they reached the crest of the motorway that looked down onto the city of Newcastle, the sky was a bright orange, it was clear for them to see that large parts of the city were burning. They stood silent and motionless as they watched the display. The brightness of the flames against the tallest buildings cast shadows that danced and moved against the clouds that had come over them during their walk. "I read somewhere that a modern city couldn't burn like this. I guess they were wrong!" Tom said. Neither John or Paul replied, they simply turned and carried on heading South.

As the night wore on and dawn threatened to catch them up they decided to take cover and rest for the day. On the junction with the A1 and the A19 they spotted a road-side café and headed in to it. Once they had checked to make sure it was clear of any stray animals or people they barricaded themselves inside and settled in for the day.

Dr Andrew Richards had been assigned to Whitehall to evaluate any possible threat to Earth from outer space. He had been given this job to sideline him away from his usual tasks advising the British government on matters of national security and where possible threats to security could come from outside the usual terrorist cells and lone gunmen with grudges against the general population. He had been sidelined because his views had proved to be controversial he didn't stand too much for the 'Normal procedures and political games' played by his colleagues whose biggest interests seemed to be career progression; even it meant ditching their own findings and conclusions to keep some *suit-wearing pen-pusher* happy *(which is how Dr Richards had described the man who had given him his latest job).*

But after November 25th he was all that was left of the whole structure as far as he knew. He had been at the army base to evaluate the effectiveness of conventional weapons; the tank he had been in was heavily camouflaged and hidden, waiting for pretend enemy tanks to come by in a war games scenario. Part of the exercise was to show how the ventilation system on the tank could withstand chemical and biological warfare but when the other participants hadn't shown and Alec couldn't get a reply from Ops they had sat very still as their training had told them to do. They had sat in the tank for forty-eight hours before the message had come over the short wave to take Dr Richards to Whitehall. It seemed that his *nothing* assignment was now the most important one there was but after the tank had grounded they had left it behind carrying on the journey in an abandoned car until they had reached the blocked road forcing them to continue on foot.

Dr Richards — or Andy as he preferred to be called — *(another reason he didn't fit in, he wasn't bothered about being referred to as Dr like so many of his peers, in fact he plain didn't like it)* now found himself in a home furnishing store in a large shopping complex just off the A1 hiding the day away while his two companions from the tank, Privates Shaw and Davies, had gone looking for food and water. They had made it to the shopping mall just as the day had started to show itself, now with the Prof *(as the two privates called him)* secured, they had gone for supplies.

As the day drew on Andy relaxed in a made-up bedroom scene, like the ones you see in all home furnishing stores that are supposed to represent real bedrooms in real houses, *(of course they don't because these bedrooms are the size*

of the houses themselves) but this didn't matter
anymore; in fact all of life's little frustrations
didn't matter anymore, the only thing that did
was getting to his destination but that would
have to wait until the sun went down again and
the rejects, animals and people alike went to
their resting places.

Andy was resting on a large king-sized bed
when he heard the first scream. He could tell
instantly it was one of the tank crew that had
brought him this far. He jumped up from the
bed and made his way to the large glass doors
that he had locked behind them earlier that day.
Pulling up the floor lock he reached up to pull
down the top one, and that was when he saw
the first crew man round the corner from the
electrical store past the customer information
desk. It was Private Davies and Andy could tell
by the look of sheer panic on his face that
something was not right.

"Open the door, Prof, open the door!"

Andy pulled down the last lock and pulled the
glass door towards him.

"They're coming, shit, they're coming!"

"What is?" Andy shouted back at him. As he
did Private Shaw followed round past the same
store and as with his friend, who was now
almost at the door, his face was fixed with
terror and now Andy could now see why.

Private Shaw or, Terry as his friends knew
him, was digging deep. His legs felt as though

they were on fire and his stomach was knotted and twisted. The heavy uniform now felt like lead and he had long ago dropped the food and water they had gone for. His heavy boots designed to keep his feet safe in the enclosed environment of the tank now acted like anchors; planting his feet firmly to the floor and making every step back up harder and harder, it was as if he was having a dream, he had to escape something but his feet felt heavy and cumbersome almost as if he was trying to run through treacle. But the clattering of claws on the highly-polished floor of the mall kept him running for his life; he could see the door to the shop and he could see Andy and Private Davies standing hurrying him up trying to wave him through the door but now he was exhausted and he could tell by the sounds behind him, the sounds of breathing and growling, that his attackers were almost on him. Then he felt the first bite and a burning hot pain shot through his left calf muscle. His leg buckled instantly and he went down, tumbling and sprawling, hitting the hard tiles head first; his nose burst on impact and as he skidded along the polished floor scattering the discarded phones and I.D.s left behind, he felt another bite, this one was in his other leg. He let out a scream of pain, tears welled up in his eyes and his nose now ran with blood and mucus. He turned himself onto his back ready to fight and defend himself but it was useless; the pack were on him. He swung at one of the dogs, catching it square in the jaw; it was sent sprawling and howling in pain but instantly his arm was grabbed and pulled back by another. These dogs had the same look in their eyes as the dogs John and his friends had seen eating the hand while they sat in the tank and as with those dogs these had clumps of fur missing, their eyes looked empty and soulless, their ears were covered with dry blood. Their movements, whilst stiff and rigid, were purposeful and they acted like a pack. In fact, it seemed to Andy, who now watched helplessly from inside the shop, that they acted in unison. Terry kicked out catching another one of the dogs in the side and again it yelped in pain but instantly turned and bit down hard just above his boot; its teeth burying deep into the soft flesh above his ankle. He was now exhausted. Both legs were now being held down and bitten with a frenzied ferocity, his left arm too was held fast and his right arm had been torn at the shoulder, now useless it lay next to him; he was unable to take out his side arm, he could do nothing now but scream in agony until the largest of the dogs took him by the throat. With one swift wrench Terry felt its teeth tear through it and as he lay on the polished cream marble floor; the life now bleeding from him; he could feel their tongues lapping at the open wounds. He felt weaker now as if on the crest of sleep and then everything went black and Terry's movements stopped.

As early evening turned into night John, Paul and Tom left the road-side café and started South through the smashed wreckage. Again, there seemed to be no end in sight to it and John imagined the road being blocked until he got home. They travelled in silence that night, all of them too exhausted to talk about trivial things and TV shows they may have seen and they were hungry — god they were hungry — although they had taken refuge in the café all of its food had spoilt; even the frozen food had long since defrosted and rotted where it still sat. Only the sealed packets of chocolates and sweets had given them any kind of sugar or calorie intake.

The night seemed to drag on, one step followed by another, their shoulders slumped and heads down they looked exactly what they were: refugees. But not from a war-torn country that had endured years of unrest at the hands of some dictator or that had been at war with itself; no, this was in Britain — the 4th richest country in the world but that was now long gone, in a matter of weeks all of our infrastructure, everything that had made living here trouble-free and secure had gone. They were refugees but they were refugees of mankind!

Eventually they saw the shape of the large

shopping mall loom out of the night's sky. John stopped and turned towards it, "It'll be day soon enough, there isn't much past here now until we get to some services further up the road but we won't make them by dawn. I think we should call in there until night fall."

Paul nodded in agreement, "I think you're right," Tom said.

They headed up the off-ramp and down towards the main building, electing to leave the surrounding retail units in favour of the main complex. It seemed to them there would be a greater chance of food in there than the smaller shops and anyway, most of them were stationary suppliers or toy shops. They pushed through the main doors and headed down the central gallery area past the false gardens with the waterfall and large plastic *Star Trek* planet rocks and round towards the stairs and escalators that would take the eager shoppers up to yet more *retail experiences* as it is — or was fashionable — to call them; and more opportunities to spend money or build up their credit card balance.

"Halt!" A voice came from ahead of them.

"Who are you?" They stopped dead.

"Who are *you?*" John replied.

"I'm Private Davies. I'm here with…" John interrupted him, "Are you the gunner from the tank that's stuck back up the road?"

There was a short silence. "I'm the loader, how

do you know about that?"

Tom took this question, "Because we have just come from there two days ago. Alec told us about you, he told us he sent you and another onwards to escort a scientist to Whitehall. Is he still with you?" Another silence followed, then a man came into view from a small clothing shop twenty yards ahead of them.

"They were, but Terry…Private Shaw the gunner was attacked yesterday and killed."

John stepped forward, "Attacked by who…a reject?"

"They were rejects but they weren't human rejects, they were dogs, a damn pack of them, he had no chance; couldn't even draw his side arm, they were on him so quickly."

"What about the scientist?" John pushed the question.

"Yeah, he's still here. I've got him safe back down there." The private pointed towards the large department store on the corner and then continued, "you'd all best come with me, it's safe in there, we have it locked down."

John started towards the private and Tom and Paul followed. He lead them towards the main entrance doors of the shop where a tall man in his late fifties stood waiting by the door. He was almost completely bald with stubble that was very quickly becoming a beard around his face. His once immaculate white shirt was now creased and dirty and the top buttons were open. John figured he must have discarded his tie a long time ago. The black trousers he had on showed signs of being slept in and dirt no doubt collected from walking and being inside the tank for as long as was. He ushered them through the door and locked it behind them as the private followed them in. Private Davies turned to the three stragglers he had found.

"I'm Private Davies, or Mathew, but call me Matt and this is the Prof."

John replied in the way that is usual in these situations

"I'm John and this is Paul and Tom." But he quickly cut short any lingering *getting to know you and how are you?* conversations before turning to the Prof, as Matt had called him, "Alec tells me you know what's happened here."

Andy smiled, "Why don't we go and sit down, I'm not sure what Alec has already told you but I'll gladly tell you what I know."

The five men made their way through to the lounge furnishings department and as John, Tom, Paul and Andy sat down and made themselves comfortable on one of the large corner suits, Matt left them and headed back to the window to stand watch. Tom spoke first as he often did. "So, Professor…" Andy cut him off, "I'm not a Professor as such, I'm a Dr of…well that doesn't matter anymore now does it? Just call me Andy, please."

John started this time, "Okay, Andy tell me exactly what is going on, why is this happening? It seems like a nightmare and I want to know if I'll see my wife and son again?" "And me too, my wife I mean, Lynne," Tom added. Andy sat further back and crossed his legs placing his clasped hands on his knee. He looked at the three men that now sat before him; all of them looked tired and weary; the exhaustion was evident on their faces as much as it was on him. He sighed and drew breath ready to tell them what he knew, he saw no reason now to hold anything back. The official secrets act seemed not to apply now and anyway, who was going to report him and to who? And if this is as he did believe it to be, the beginning of the end of the human race, surely they had a right to know....didn't they?

Chapter Six
The Truth

Andy started, "Okay, for decades now we've believed, known, that we're not alone and all of the major governments around the world have known it as well, but the thing is we could never let it be common knowledge and for all that time governments have been able to keep a lid on it discounting so-called video footage as hoaxes or even weather balloons, but with the advances in technology it's becoming harder and harder to do this."

"What do you mean, technology?" Tom asked.

"Well, almost everybody now has a camera phone or a camcorder and PC. Years ago with film or even video tape images were so grainy it was easy to just dismiss it but now the keenest amateurs can produce very high quality images so it's becoming simply too hard to just casually disregard them."

"So when was the big reveal going to happen?" Andy turned to Paul and started to smile.

"It already has started, have you noticed how many books and movies have been released lately about alien invasions and in most of them how we, as a joint human race, manage to beat them back and be triumphant?"

"So, that's just because Hollywood knows it

sells?" John remarked.

" No, it's not, it's because they're preparing the psyche, they're getting you used to the idea, that's how it's done; it's happened all through modern history, you don't think the American military would simply just hand over e-mail and the internet do you? They've been manipulated for years to get us used to things. Had this event not happened, next year would have been the time we would have started to leak information out."

"How?"

"By the usual methods, not some big announcement by the PM but by subversive means, like leaving documents on a train or a bus, the odd laptop in a pub and leaking stuff to the press and on the web by making it easy for hackers to gain access to certain databases and files, believe me there a plenty of ways of getting information out without people knowing it's actually happening."

Andy sat further back and sighed again, his eyes were tired and drawn. "But of course we didn't get the chance, we just didn't see this coming."

John pushed forward on his seat and leaned towards him.

"How could you not have seen this? I mean, satellites and the telescope...what's it called?"

"Hubble," Tom answered him.

Andy nodded very slightly, "Most satellites

are designed to look in over not out into space and anyway even the ones that do look at about 10% of the sky the majority spy on us. The ones up there that are for spying that is, and it's not as many as you might think, most of them up there spinning around above us are for communications, weather, TV and that sort of thing and as for the Hubble; it's designed for deep space. It simply is unable to focus on anything close to us, it can't even be focused on the moon, don't you think if it could it would have taken shots of the abandoned Moon landers, buggies and flags and put an end to the whole *did they didn't they?* argument? And anyway, no matter what we have up there or down here; if anything approaches from the sun we just wouldn't see it."

"There is another problem though isn't there," Tom started and continued, "what about religion? I mean, suddenly we're not alone; that would blow open the whole *were we made* or was it purely by chance and evolution debate."

Andy sat back again, his throat felt sore and thick.

"Religion wouldn't have been the big problem. Remember, most religions came about when mankind was looking for answers to questions we simply weren't able to answer. Why does the sun rise and set in the same place? Why does the sea come in and out? Why do birds migrate at the same time every year? Why do crops fail some years and not others? I mean, shit, we didn't even know which questions to ask so we had no chance of finding the answer!"

"So what would have been the biggest problem?" John asked.

"Social order, which is of course very close to religion, in fact they are inseparable, you have to understand that even those who don't believe in a god live by a moral code that came from religion, you know, *thou shall not kill* and the deadly sins etcetera. Put simply without religion we simply wouldn't have it and we wouldn't have gotten as far in becoming as civilised as we have.

"Yeah, but come on, I'm an atheist but I live by a moral code. Anybody that wants to be part of society does."

John interrupted but Andy shook his head in frustration, "You're missing the point, you might live by the moral code expected of you in a modern society but go back a few thousand years…who do you think wrote it? Like it or not we all live by it…well, with the odd exception, of course."

The four men sat in silence for a moment. What had happened in the last few weeks was just too much to deal with and now in this quiet, safe and comfortable setting it was all starting to sink in and it was a feeling that none of them liked.

As the sun grew higher in the December sky and the light shone through the large glass panels in the ceiling in the main mall outside the shop windows, they could feel the fatigue start to gain control again, but John wouldn't give up, he had too many questions he needed answering.

"So what now? I mean, do you know what had actually happened or is it all guess work?"

Andy shook his head, "No, it's not guess work, we know pretty much what has happened and I can give you an educated guess as what is next for us."

"So what's the answer?" John pushed Andy even though he could tell he was becoming more uncomfortable. He looked between them, again moving in his seat as he did and running his hand over his head, the three of them could tell he felt very uncomfortable but they weren't going to let him off easy.

"So!" Tom pushed again.

"The rain, we don't know how they did it but they put the whole planet to sleep, everybody above the water line or that wasn't in a sealed environment blacked out, it was done on a global scale."

"But you said you knew something was coming, why didn't you prepare?" Paul asked.

"Because we simply didn't have time, the first clues came from the ISS."

"What's that?" Tom asked.

"The *International Space Station*, we lost communications with it approximately fifteen-minutes before the rain started."

"Didn't they see anything?" Andy turned back to face John.

"It wasn't designed as a castle keep for the Earth, they had no warning. They reported nothing unusual, they just went off air, so to speak."

"So what do you think has happened to them?"

Andy shrugged his shoulders, "No-one knew. I was having a conversation with our space agency when they too went off air. Since then we've heard once over the short wave which was the order to get me to Whitehall. Truth is, if I get there I don't know if anybody else will."

Tom sat forward, "But I don't get it, you told us all these books and movies about aliens coming down and attacking us were to prepare us for the eventual admission of life out there," Tom pointed in a general upwards direction, "but that's not what happened is it? They didn't come down and fight us."

"No they didn't, and I think the reason for that is even though their technology must be far in advance of ours they must have decided not to fight. I guess we could have given them a bloody nose and of course there is the..." Andy stopped and shifted again.

"There is the what?" John asked.

"It's called the *Final Resolution Protocol.* If the Earth was to be taken over and all hope was lost, the governments that have them would fire all of their land and sea-based nuclear warheads at key points around the globe; making it uninhabitable for anyone — human or alien."

"Shit!" John fell back into his seat and Andy looked amongst them; again they all had the same expression and it was one absolute disbelief.

"You're telling me that best plan our government came up with if we lost a war with little green men would be to blow up the fucking planet?"

Andy shrugged his shoulders and smiled but it was a smile of acceptance at what he had just told them. "Yes, if mankind had lost a battle with...little green men," he pointed at John, "then the only hope we would ever have to repel them would be to make the very thing they came for no use to them, otherwise what would be the fate of us, slaves? Sub servants? Tell me what would you prefer?"

No answer came from any of them and Andy continued, "The fact is this, even if there are more people like us, I estimate that there is likely to be only around 7-8 million people left worldwide and they won't last very long."

John shook his head and cut across him, "No, no, no. The Earth's population has been that low before and mankind built it up."

Andy responded with a similar shaking of his head, "It's not the same, the last time the population was this low people were used to hunting, gathering and building shelters; living off the land and outside, its skills the vast majority of the population have lost and forgotten; hell it's so rare they make TV show's out of it now for Christ's sake."

Tom interrupted him, "But we already have shelters, there are plenty of houses empty and food in the supermarkets. I mean, we could live off that for years."

No! no we couldn't. The houses have no heating, most now have central heating or at least heating that's dependant on a mains supply and without the gas or electricity supplies they will soon become mould and damp-infected and once they start to crumble they'll be simply too unsafe to life in. As for the food, even tinned food has an expiration date of around a year so there maybe plenty of stock but it will be inedible very soon, sooner than you think in fact. And what about water? Again, bottled water will go off eventually because of the treatments it's gone through then where will your drinking water come from? The taps? That will stop very soon if it hasn't already with no sewage treatments it will all back-spill into rivers and streams or simply leak out through broken pipes that will no longer be replaced. As for fresh water do you know how to tell if water from a stream or lake is safe to drink?"

"Oh, come on, our ancestors didn't check water," Tom argued.

"No they didn't but then their ancestors hadn't been pumping sewage and chemical waste into it for years and years."

Andy broke off and rubbed his hands together, gripping them into a tight fist before he continued, "And then there's disease. Believe it or not we have far more of them now. Super bugs — brought about by our own antibiotics mutant colds and flus, all kept at bay by medicines and drugs that also have a finite shelf life."

"But we could build the numbers back up," John said.

"Really, John? You're looking for your wife and son, yes? And you Tom, you're looking for your wife? So even though you don't know what's happened to them and you're still feeling saddened and hurt you would reproduce with the first woman you met now? The social order we're so proud of, the thing that defines us as humans simply wouldn't allow reproduction in the way we used to. When mankind started off we bred much like most primates do but now we don't; now we enter *(for the most part)* into loving monogamous-based relationships and with the population being so low and spread out it will become one of our greatest disadvantages. Believe me, we've run these scenarios for years and it's always the same outcome. Once the human race drops below a certain level we go the same way as the Dinosaurs and nothing can change that, not now. Put simply gentlemen our time has come and gone."

Andy stood up and walked around the area of the store they sat in; stretching as he did, John, Paul and Tom sat silently staring at the floor, almost unable to take in what they had been told so far. Then John looked back up at Andy, "You still haven't told us the most important thing yet, have you?"

Andy sighed again, he felt so drained he was worn out, past being tired he was running now on pure reserve energy, he had come to terms with the fact that he would never see Whitehall or in fact the outside of this building, what was the point? He knew the truth, he knew what the inevitable outcome would be, if a reject didn't get him, it would be either starvation or some sort of infection. The cities were already becoming no-go areas the un-emptied bins and rotting food in all the homes, office blocks and shops were attracting animals and by the far the biggest invasion came from the rats; even some of the body parts left by the sides of smashed cars were now gourmet food for crows and other scavengers. No, the cities were now deserts, a place to be avoided at all costs, they would simply become too dangerous to be in and over time they would crumble and turn back into the land they were built on.

John asked again and Andy knew he had to answer. "Tell us, what do you think has happened to everyone, why are all their phones and I.D.s lying where they were?"

Alex sat back in his chair and cleared his throat.

"Look at the clues, they put the world to sleep, they took everyone they could and then left leaving behind everything we would need to identify or contact each other, they didn't come here to conquer us or take our planet for themselves, they came here for something else, something that can only be found on this small, little insignificant rock."

"Us," Tom whispered.

"Us," Andy confirmed.

"I don't get it, what do mean they came for us?" John asked.

"Think about it, when you harvest a crop do you destroy the field afterwards or just take the wheat and leave?"

Tom interrupted again, "Well, you take the wheat, of course."

Andy smiled at him, "Then you know the answer, it's been a harvest for them and we're the crop."

John looked at Andy, his mouth started to

form the question he didn't want an answer to, but then he didn't want any of this but now he had to know, he had to know if his worst fears would be confirmed by Andy, a man that in any other life he would never have met, but now here in this life his answer could change John's world from the frightening reality it is now into an unimaginable nightmare from which there would simply be no escape. As these thoughts ran through his mind and a cold sweat ran down his back, followed almost instantly by the adrenaline his body was now pumping around him ready to handle inevitable, he asked the question, "So what do you think they would want to take us for?"

Andy's face was full of sorrow, his eyes had watered as he watched John form the question. He knew what he was about to ask him and he knew John didn't want to ask it anymore than Andy wanted to answer it, but it had to be this way; there could be no grey areas; these travellers needed to know what he knew, he took in a deep breath and looked John dead in the eyes.

"Why do we harvest wheat?"

Tom answered the question that didn't need to be with a softly spoken whisper that was full of sorrow and dismay.

"To eat it!"

Chapter Seven
The Journey Home

An uneasy silence had come over them since Tom had answered Andy's last question and the monster in John's mind had burst free, painting vivid images of Sam and Mickey fighting to be free; even though he had no idea what from or where from but it didn't matter; the thought of his wife and son being *harvested* like some crop in a farmer's field was enough for the monster to take full control of his imagination and the images he was seeing made him feel like his head would simply implode at any moment.

Eventually John managed to cage it again and push the pictures and thoughts away with it, and as the three men struggled to accept what they had been told, outside the first snows of the winter had started to fall and with it the temperatures.

As Andy watched the snow build up on the glass roof in the main mall he knew that any other survivors caught out in it wouldn't last the night and his predictions and worst fears about mankind's survivability would start to be proven. He turned and headed back towards the rear of the store and the bedroom displays. Matt had fallen asleep in the bed he had dragged over to the entrance and the three travellers had each taken to a bed one by one; falling into a deep and much-needed sleep. Watching them it hit Andy again just how tired he was. Climbing into the bed he had used since they had arrived, it didn't take him long to fall asleep with them.

As darkness descended once again John, Paul and Tom started to wake from the longest and by far most comfortable sleep they had had since this event had happened. Andy and Matt were already up talking quietly by the entrance as John approached them. Andy turned towards him, "How are you feeling after your sleep?" he asked.

"A little better I guess but of course now I'm awake I have to face up to what you told me earlier and to be honest I'd rather have not woken up."

Andy smiled at him. It was about all he could do, what could he say? He couldn't *un-tell* him and even if he could he wouldn't. John and his friends had to make the right choices now and Andy believed firmly that you can only do that once you have all the facts or at least as many as there were available.

During that night they scavenged the shopping mall taking winter cloths, back packs, torches along with food and water for their inevitable journey further South. They enjoyed a warm wash and shave courtesy of the camping stoves they had liberated from the outside pursuits shop. The plan was simple: use this night to prepare and gather all the equipment they would need to make it safely home and the following day to rest and gather the strength they would also need.

Day once again turned back to night and it was time to go, time to set out into the winter's night and head home. "One final push," John thought to himself as they put on the cold weather gear and picked up their heavy bag packs.

As they started to head towards the door Tom stopped and dropped his pack.

"What are you doing?" asked John.

Tom looked at the ground and then back at him with a look of defeat in his eyes.

"I'm not going," he replied.

"What?"

"I'm staying here with Andy and Matt. It's obvious I'm not going to see Lynne again I know that now. In fact, I've known it since I first saw what had happened after you'd found me, but until we met Andy I couldn't bring myself to admit it, now I can; now I know that this is it."

Tom walked over to him and placed his hand on John's shoulder.

"You go on."

"You're sure about this?"

Tom smiled at him, "I am, you go on you find your Sam and Mickey, you never know they may have been missed and maybe they're waiting for you now at home."

John smiled back at Tom and nodded, "You take care Tom, it was a pleasure."

Tom moved his hand down and extended it out, John took it firmly and shook hands one last time with him.

"Okay let's go," John said, as he turned to Paul. Tom gestured to him and Paul waved his hand back then turned and followed John out through the doors into the darkness of the shopping mall.

Outside Andy and Matt waited for them.

"Thanks for everything, Andy," John said.

"I'm not sure what *everything* is but you're welcome,"

he replied smiling.

"The shelter, the clothes and the truth," Paul replied.

"Here's something else," Matt said and he held out the 9mm pistol that had belonged to Private Shaw. John took it from him and pushed it down into his coat pocket.

"You fired one before?" Matt asked him.

"A while ago, we were working in Texas so it seemed the thing to do."

The four men shook hands and then separated. Andy and Matt walked back into the store and locked the doors behind them. John and Paul headed out past the now dried blood; that was all that was left of Private Shaw and through the main doors into the dead of night.

Outside was quiet, the snow that had fallen had brought an eerie and uneasy peace, no sounds could be heard; it was absolute silence. The clear sky of the night allowed the snow to glisten and sparkle as it froze where it had landed covering everything, turning the scene of the sharp twisted metal frames that formed the carnage on the motorways and roads to a soft white unspoilt landscape of peace and tranquillity. The snow crunched beneath their feet as John and Paul made their way South once again thankful for their new purposefully-made clothing that would, without doubt, save their lives now winter had taken its grip on the UK.

As they rounded the A1 and started to head up Lobley Hill they could see the Angel of The North standing against the backdrop of the black sky. Snow had fallen and settled along her wings and though John and Andy had passed her many times on their travels, tonight she seemed to have special significance.

"Wouldn't it be good if she could see us home safe?" Paul said, as they passed beneath the metal structure. But both men knew that the statue could not help them, now they were on their own and they had to make as much time as they could before the night started to slip away.

They reached Durham before day started to break through. They had headed for the road-side services that John had used a few times whilst passing this way. Pushing through the glass doors, that would no longer operate automatically, they stamped the snow off their feet and headed inside past the usual stores and video game areas towards the restaurants at the back. It was as cold inside as it was outside. They decided to erect the tent they had taken along with the other gear to keep them warm and at least somewhat protected. Inside John lit the camping stove and boiled the water needed for their dehydrated food. After eating, both men settled down into their sleeping bags and as day broke through the windows, illuminating the tent inside to a bright yellow, they drifted into a restless and uncomfortable sleep.

It was Paul that awoke to the sounds coming from outside the tent. A shuffling sound that was periodically replaced with sniffing and snorting. Paul reached over and shook John, who started to wake to find him standing over him with his finger on his lips, "Shhhh, there's something outside the tent."

John slowly climbed out of his bag and started to listen. Again the shuffling sound came and again it was followed by sniffing and snorting.

"What is that?" Paul whispered.

John replied by shaking his head. He moved

over to the tent flap and slowly started to pull the zip down. His hand shook with the apprehension he was feeling about what might be out there, what was it this time? They had seen men and dogs that had reacted to the rain but he knew there were many other animals that may well have become free and that could also have been affected and Tom's comments about the zoos now flashed back into his mind with absolute clarity.

The zip was now half-way down and all sounds outside the tent had stopped. John pushed his head through the gap and looked around the interior of the services but he could see nothing. Whatever it was that had been sniffing around the tent had now gone. He turned back in to face Paul. "There's nothing out there," he said, pulling the zip further down. He stepped out, closely followed by Paul, now both men scoured the services; it was still daylight though neither knew what the time was, they hadn't seen the need to keep time since this had first started. That along with almost everything they knew, or had made into habits, seemed to belong to another distant — almost past life.

"What do you think we should do?" Paul asked.

"I don't know about you but I need the toilet," he said, as he pulled his coat on and set off in the direction of the public toilets, closely followed by Paul. Once inside both men entered a cubicle and out of an old world habit locked the doors.

Within seconds the main door into the *Gents* started to squeak as it was pushed open and the unmistakable sound of claws against a hard tiled floor could be heard by both of them. They could hear it pass along the rows of cubicles towards the far end of the toilets and then stop. Both men were breathing as quietly as they could. Adrenaline once again started to pump around them as the white hot feeling of fear ran down their spines.

They listened as the sniffing and snorting started again; followed by the tap, tap, tapping of the claws as it walked back down the line of cubicles right to the two that John and Paul occupied; then the tapping stopped and whatever it was stood outside, separated only by the thin compressed wooden door and a single flimsy metal lock.

John stood as far away from the door as he could. Standing with the toilet now between his legs and his back pressed hard against the cold tiled wall. As he moved his hands up his right hand passed in front of the toilet flush detector; the water started to flow, the noise it produced in the silence seemed to be a thousand times louder than it usually was. Instantly the growling and snarling started as the animal started to attack. He could hear it scratching at the door. Its teeth snapping together between growls and he knew that if he didn't react fast it would get in and there simply wasn't enough room in the tiny cubicle for him to defend himself; he would have to do something.

"Paul, you still in there? You still got the door locked?"

"Where the fuck do you think I'll be?" came the reply and John could tell from his anxious reply and the tremor in his voice Paul was just as terrified as he was.

"Okay, I'm coming over." John stood on the toilet and climbed over the thin wall into Paul's cubicle.

"Okay, so now what? Now were both trapped in here."

Paul's words were no more steady than the last.

"Hold onto my belt and pull me back when I say," John said.

Standing on the toilet again pulling himself up and leaning over the wall he reached down to the door lock that was still holding the animal out, fumbling for it he managed to slide the lock up, instantly it burst through the door charging into the cubicle and hitting the wall.

Dazed, it fell, scrambling to get back to its feet. John knew that he had seconds for his plan to work. He slammed the door shut behind it and slid the lock back down trapping the large black dog inside.

"Pull me now!" John screamed and Paul did with all his strength. John fell back into the cubicle and on top of Paul.

"Now what?" Paul shouted.

John turned to him as he pulled the lock on their cubicle across. "Now we fucking run!" Both men charged out of the cubicle and through the main door out of the toilet block.

"What was it?" asked Paul, as they ran back through the services towards the tent and their supplies.

"Some kind of a dog — a big black dog — I didn't wait to see exactly what type and to be honest I don't give a fuck; let's just get out of here before it gets out or his friends come."

"But what about the tent and supplies?" Paul asked.

"Leave them, they're no good to us if we've been ripped limb from limb," came the reply, and Paul could tell he wasn't open to a discussion on the matter; whatever they leave behind will stay there.

"When we came in I noticed a pick-up truck half out of the parking bay. I bet it has the keys in it."

Paul shouted as he tried to keep up with John, "It's no use in this snow, we'll just get stuck."

"No," Paul replied, and then continued, "it's a 4x4 it should be okay."

The two men reached the glass entrance doors and pulled them open as they had done to get in that morning. Once they had pushed through the door John started to pull them closed.

"What are doing?" Paul asked him.

"I don't want them getting out."

Now outside with only their coats for protection, having left everything else inside, they realised how vulnerable they now were. The snow had continued to fall and as it did so had the temperatures.

"Where's this pick-up?"

Paul pointed to his left, the truck was exactly how he had described it, half out of its parking bay. The wipers stopped in mid sweep, no doubt trying to clear the purple rain when its driver had succumb to it.

"I hope you're right Paul, we won't last a night out here or back in there," John said, as they walked over to it.

Grabbing the driver's door he pulled it open and there from the ignition lock hung the keys: "Thank Christ!" he said. He reached in and turned them. The engine fired into life.

"Get in." Paul climbed into the passenger seat and both men sat with the doors closed and sighed with relief.

All the windows on the pick-up were frozen over and covered with snow.

"What now?" Paul asked.

John turned to him, "Well, I'm not going back in there to get some de-icer," he said, as he pointed back towards the services. "We sit here until the engine warms up then we can clear the windows with the heater and a scraper."

"What scraper?" Paul replied.

John grinned and pulled his wallet out. Opening it up he took out his platinum credit card. "This'll do nicely," he said, with a rare smile across his face.

Paul laughed back at him and did the same. "Mine's only a gold card though." "You'll have to travel in the back then."

Both men shared a laugh. It had seemed a life time ago since they had done that. Over the last few weeks there had been no reasons to laugh or smile and really there wasn't now but something in them allowed them to share a little moment of happiness; maybe it was a self-preservation response, something the mind did to stop it from collapsing completely. They had heard of people laughing at funerals or at times when it seemed completely inappropriate to do so but whatever the reason was it helped and both of them felt a new urgency and a new drive to get home.

Hot air now blew out of the vents filling the cab of the pick-up with a warmth that was very welcome and that they knew would keep them alive. After scraping the windows clear and discarding their credit cards to the ground they both climbed back in.

"That was one expensive window clean!" John continued with the good humour that had found them. Paul chuckled and with that John engaged the four wheel drive and pointed the pick-up towards the exit and the south bound lane.

The drive was a slow one, around 15mph was as fast as John dared to go. The wipers worked furiously to keep the windows clear of the falling snow but even then, weaving in and out of the now covered wrecks was proving difficult. Paul pulled the glove box open and started to look through it. He pulled out the owner's mobile phone and pushed the power button. The screen lit up along with the usual chime to say *I'm on.*

"It's working?" John asked as he stared through the white-out that now faced him outside the window.

"Seems so," Paul replied.

"Let's see if it'll get a connection."

But as with the other phones they had found and tried along the way it didn't; it was nothing now but a plastic paperweight just like all the phones that were left behind. He threw it back into the glove box and slammed it shut.

Eventually they reached the junction that would take them East and across to the link road that would lead to John's home. The truck's lights blazed through the snow fall that had lightened from the blizzard but was still falling slowly. They trundled along the back roads as they passed under the bridge that carried the main eastern rail line. They came upon what had once been a high speed train, but now, as with everything else, it was nothing but a smashed empty object that now belonged to a former world and life. Just pieces of metal, glass and plastic laying across the embankment where it had derailed, tumbling down the bank before it had smashed into the very bridge that had once carried it.

They past it slowly, both of them looking at the great hulk wondering what had became of the people inside, did anyone survive the crash or had anyone been missed?

Every once in a while they would feel a little bump and they knew that another discarded phone that had been covered by the snow had now been crushed by the truck. The road seemed to be endless; they were used to it but they were used to travelling it at much higher speeds. Usually by this time of the year they were home, laid off until spring, so they didn't have to travel in the worst of the winter months.

As they reached the crest of the road that had brought them closer to home they came to Stockton on Tees, the nearest town to John. With an estimated population of 190,000 people the roads through the town are usually busy, especially this time of the year *(though neither of them knew the exact date — they knew it was late December)* but as with everywhere it was a desolate and frozen ghost town.

Nothing moved and as night fell the street lights remained dark along with traffic lights and homes and offices.

They continued through the town past the quay side and the river Tees which was frozen solid. The boats that normally travelled up and down it for pleasure were stuck fast where they were.

John carefully charted the truck past the large retail units and out of the town centre towards his home village.

Five hours had passed since they had left the services behind. John knew he was on the last part of his journey and that hopefully he would soon see his home. Now he was convinced more than ever that he would find Sam and Mickey waiting for him like they always did when he came home on leave.

Outside the mirrors of the pick-up and the parts of the windows that didn't directly receive any heat had started to freeze again; even the wipers had frozen to the glass but inside the constant stream of hot air kept them warm and protected form the sub zero temperatures outside; as they headed through the last large population centre before they would enter the country roads that would lead

John to his home village.

Something caught Paul's attention, something in the corner of his eye, just in the beam of the pick-up's headlamps.

"What was that?" he asked.

"What?" John replied.

Paul pointed to his left, "Over there, it looked like a person laying in the snow."

"A reject?" John replied.

"I don't think so, remember what Alec said? they go in long before it's dark."

"So maybe this one didn't make it."

"No I don't think so," Paul insisted and continued, "if this had laid here since light he would have been covered by the snow fall earlier."

John squeezed the brakes on the pick-up, bringing it to a stop. Now only the diesel engine and the sound of the ventilation broke the eerie silence.

"What now?" John asked impatiently.

"I need to look. I need to see if they're like us, you know, normal."

"And if they're not, if they're a reject then what?"

Paul sat back and undid his seat belt, "There's two of us and I have a torch."

John sighed and stepped out of the cab with Paul into the freezing air. He left the truck running to keep it warm and for a quick getaway if needed but in these conditions even with four wheel drive, a quick getaway seemed unlikely.

The two men approached the now still body that lay on top of the freshly fallen snow wearing nothing but a plain white shirt and black suit trousers. They could see as they approached by the torch light that he was face up and a man in his mid-thirties. Both of them approached with a feeling of trepidation. They had nearly made it to the relative safety of John's cottage; if they were beaten now what was the point in trying at all?

John suddenly remembered the gift from Matt and reached into his pocket. Pulling out the 9mm pistol he had given him, releasing the safety, he pointed the gun towards the still figure.

"Jesus! Where did you get that?" Paul asked him.

"Matt gave me it, it belonged to the other tank crew, the one that was killed."

Paul regained his composure and they reached the feet of the man. He started to shine the torch light up his body towards his face and as the light hit it Paul jumped and then trembled at what he saw. The man was a reject but he looked different to the two they had seen before. His face looked bloated, swollen, and disproportionate to his body. Blood had ran from every orifice on his head but it was dark red, almost black.

Paul knelt down beside him placing his hand on his chest. As he did it heaved and the man's eyes rolled towards them. Paul sprang back and John pointed the gun at his head but the reject didn't move. A slow breath escaped his mouth, combined with a strained moan, almost like a cry for help. Paul couldn't help but feel sad for him. He had noticed that the man had a wedding ring on his left hand; that meant he once had a family and now with them, god knows where he was laying in the snow having been affected and turned by the rain and both Paul and John knew that these heavy slow breaths were the breaths on a dying man.

"What do we do?" Paul asked.

John shook his head, "I don't know."

As they stood and watched another slow breath leave him, his chest heaved one last time and then stopped. His gaze moved away from them as his eyes rolled back into his head.

"Do you think it was being out at night?" Paul asked again.

"No and I don't think it was the cold either."

What do you mean?"

John knelt down beside him and poked the end of the gun into one of the pools of the thick black, reddish blood; as he pulled it back the blood stuck to it and the man's face like a thick syrup.

"Look, reject or not, there is no way anybody can survive with blood that thick. Your organs would start to shut down and your heart would simply be unable to continue."

He stood back and turned to Paul, "What if they're dying? What if all animals that were affected by the rain die like this? It's not impossible. Whatever it was that turned them into these things could just as easily kill them as the process continues."

"Let's hope so," Paul said, as he switched the torch off and turned away back towards the truck, and as he did the man's contorted face disappeared into the night.

Back inside the warm cab John put the pick-up into gear and set off again. The large wheels trampled their way through the snow. Both men sat in silence and as they did Paul contemplated which of the three fates they had come across was the worst: surviving alone as they had, turning into a reject and dying a slow painful death as they had just witnessed, or being taken for food.

Little did Paul know that right at that moment John had the same thought process going on in his mind.

Eventually they reached the open countryside and small lanes that would lead John home. Light had started to break in the distance and as it did the desolation and blankness stretched out in front of them. The white landscape looked barren and empty, devoid of all life and it hit Paul; if this was it, if all around was deserted and even the rejects were dying off, this would be their life from now on. No-one and nothing else would come into it. It would be just the two of them until the end.

The feeling washed over Paul and for the first time since this nightmare had begun he started to feel overwhelmed; a sense of panic was growing in him he felt. No, he knew that at any moment his heart would stop with the over-powering sense of uselessness that surrounded him. A feeling of heat washed over him; his hairs stood on end and his breathing became shallow. Nausea built up in his stomach and his hands started to tremble, as they did he became light-headed and then nothing but blackness.

John hit the brakes hard when he saw Paul collapse in his seat. The Toyota Hilux skidded on the ice-covered snow to stop.

"Paul, Paul, you okay, what's wrong?"

John slapped his face on each side and his eyes started to flicker and then open.

"Shit, you scared me you bastard, what's wrong?"

Paul sat back up in his seat and hit the button to lower his window. Gulping in the cold air John could see the colour returning to his friend.

"I don't know what happened. I started to feel sick and then I guess I passed out."

John moved back over to his seat.

"Do you feel okay now?"

Paul nodded, "Yeah, I think so. I mean, yes I do."

Paul looked embarrassed but continued, "Look, I haven't told you this, but I suffer from panic attacks. I guess with everything that's happened and being so close to our journey's end it hit me all at once. I'm okay, just keep driving John, I'll be fine."

John smiled and turned his attention back to the road. He shifted into 1st gear and set off down the narrow lane. Paul gulped some more of the freezing air and then flicked the switch to raise the window back up. Once in position the warm air from the vents started to warm the cab again and Paul felt relaxed, at ease, and tranquil.

John rounded the last corner and turned right at the T-junction that will take them into Hutton Rudby.

The pick-up climbed the snow-covered bank and passed the Wheatsheaf Inn that him, Sam and Mickey would have Sunday lunch in whenever he was home.

He drove past the village green. The trees stood bare and defiant against the snow as did the flag post. They past the unmistakable snow-covered shape of two crashed cars. Just after this John stopped the truck and engaged its parking brake, turning the engine off he turned to Paul, "We're here!"

Chapter Eight
Home

John sat in the pick-up looking at his home. Now that he'd made it; now he was actually here; he seemed too frightened by what he might find *(or not find)* to actually go in but he knew he had to; he had to push down his fears one last time. He had to know if his wife and son were in there or not.

Digging deep with his adrenaline surging around him he pulled the door catch and climbed out of the truck quietly closing it door behind him. Paul did the same and rounded it to stand beside his friend.

"Should we?" Paul whispered.

John didn't reply or even acknowledge him, he simply stepped forward and started the short walk over the snow-covered grass that separated his home from the main road where he had parked. He reached the large black front door and placed his hand on the round brass handle; twisting it, the door jolted and came open.

Slowly he placed his hand on it and pushed it open, he was met with the hallway, he could see Sam and Mickey's coats hanging above the large metal radiator and Mickey's bright blue Wellington boots he had bought him on his last trip home. Taking his first step into the house he started down the hall past the first room, which was John's office, past the bottom of the staircase and into the large kitchen diner at the back of the house.

The house was cold, bitterly cold, with no power and no oil. The heating hadn't being working for a while and now he understood what Andy had meant about houses not offering the shelter and safety now the infrastructure was no longer in place.

As he entered his heart sunk. The sight that faced him was the worst one he could imagine because he knew now, without any doubt, that they had not been missed, they had not managed to avoid being taken. He knew this without doubt because all around the kitchen were the signs that Mickey's birthday party had been in full swing when the rain had come. On the large kitchen table that they would all sit around and eat at, play boards games, draw or any other family activity that they all enjoyed doing together, was the party food and cake. Now completely covered in mould and fungi. The stench was unbearable. The spilt bottles of fizzy drinks and water lay exactly where they had come to rest when the table had been knocked by the people around it falling onto it as they had succumb to the purple rain. The oven doors in the kitchen were open and the now stale pizzas, still sat on the oven grills that had been in the middle of being removed, chips lay on the floor and the oven tray that they had been in lay discarded next to them. Balloons and other party decorations had been handed the same fate as the food: left and abandoned.

John knew that had Sam survived this none of these things would have been left where they were. She would have undoubtedly tidied it all away.

John pulled one of the pine chairs up from the floor and sank into it, sighing heavily, putting his head into his hands.

Paul could see his shoulders heaving up and down and he knew John was crying for his wife and son.

"I'll go look upstairs," he said, but John didn't respond. The only sound that came from him was the soft mournful sobbing that had started almost immediately after he had sat down.

Paul turned and headed back out of the kitchen and upstairs. The large mirror at the top that John and Sam had bought when they had moved into the house caught his reflection and then attention as he passed it. Paul stood and looked back at the unrecognisable reflection that stood before him. His face was gaunt and pale and the usual sparkle in his eyes had long gone; replaced now by a sadness and dullness that made him feel his very soul had been taken from him by the events of the last few weeks.

He started forward again checking each of the

three bedrooms and the bathroom before starting back down the stairs to where he had left his friend.

John wiped his eyes clear of the salty burning tears that had ran down his face. As he did he noticed his digital video camera still attached to its tripod laying against the window seat. No doubt having been knocked over in the commotion that had taken place here and he realised that where it had been standing was directly opposite Mickey's seat. He knew that because that was where his birthday cake was with the candles now burnt down to the wick and wax covering the picture of *Optimus Prime* from his favourite film.

John flashed back to the summer when they had both sat down to watch the movie over and over again while he was home, but his thoughts soon crashed back to now, walking over to the camera he lifted it from its stand and pushed the *on* button. The little camera came to life; its battery saved from running flat by its auto standby feature; something he had insisted his new camera must have because of Sam's usual habit of not switching things off *(this had been a long running joke between them from when they had first met)*. He hit the play button and as he watched the digital playback he slumped down the wall and sat on the cold flag stones that covered the kitchen floor.

Paul came back into the kitchen to find John

still slumped on the floor. In his outstretched hands that rested on his knees he held a little blue training shoe; he clutched it tightly with his head bowed down staring at the floor beneath him.

"What's that?" was the only thing Paul could think of saying to announce his presence to John. Of course he knew what it was but he couldn't find the right words to ask what he needed to.

"Is that Mickey's? and why is it here?" is what he needed to ask; it was what he wanted to ask but he just couldn't.

John looked up at him, his eyes now sore and red and his nose ran freely with mucus but none of this seemed apparent to him. He looked in the direction of the table and Paul saw the little camera laying on it. Instantly he knew that John was referring to it. He reached across and pressed the play button that John had done only moments before.

"Mickey, wait till mummy gets the camera working. You know daddy wants to see this when he gets home tonight."

It was the unmistakable voice of Sam and on the screen he could see Mickey; his blue eyes wide with the excitement of his own birthday party and sitting next to him were his friends form the village play group. All of them staring at the large sponge birthday cake that sat in front of Mickey. Sam's arms came into view as she lit the candles on his cake, now all of the children sang, *'Happy birthday to you, happy birthday to you, happy birthday dear Mickey...happy birthday to you.'* Then a loud cheer could be heard as all the children clapped around him.

"Now get ready son." It was Sam again.

"Make a wish and Bl..." She stopped. Another voice, another mum screamed, "Did you hear that?"

"It, it sounded like a car crash," Sam replied with a concerned tone in her voice.

Another voice came from the kitchen out of shot, "Is it suppose to rain today?"

"Rain?" another voice replied.

"I hope not, my washing is out."

A crashing sound came from the kitchen followed by hysterical shouting, "Karen, Karen, are you okay? God! Karen's fainted."

Then the camera started to capture the event unfold. The parents dropped first behind the seated children; they started to drop where they stood, some falling straight down, others banging into the solid pine table.

Sam went down sideways and out of shot. The children barley managed to start to cry before one by one they too fell asleep in the chairs. Mickey went as well, his large blue eyes rolled and his head flopped forward hitting the corner of his cake.

Paul's gaze left the camera's little screen for a

second and fixed on the cake. The indent he had made was still there, now there was nothing, everything on the camera was still, only the sounds of breathing could be heard; deep slow breathing, exactly like the breathing people exhibit when they are in their deepest sleep. A beeping sound started.

"It's the oven," John said quietly, almost whispering from where he was sitting.

"Must have been the pizzas," he said in the same manner.

Paul hit the fast forward button. Nothing moved but the time on the screen until it reached 7:53pm. He saw a shadow, then another, but nothing in view. Sam had the camera so tightly zoomed in on Mickey only shapes and peripheral objects could be seen. Then suddenly something did come into view with fast purposeful and accurate movements; it was a hand — a long grey hand with only three fingers and what looked like a long opposable thumb that was almost as long as the hand itself.

Paul jumped back. His stomach twisted as his mind tried to respond to what his eyes could see. Adrenaline once again started to cause around his body and his hands shook as he tried to hold the camera still and watch this nightmare unfold.

The hand grabbed Mickey's throat and started to lift him from his seat but his feet jammed between the table and chair that he sat on. Whatever was holding him lowered him slightly and pulled again, this time faster and harder like someone trying to pull open a stuck drawer. He caught again and again but on the fourth pull he came free as his lifeless and limp legs were lifted out of shot. The little blue trainer on his right foot fell off and tumbled beneath the table.

Paul placed the camera back down on the table and turned to look at John who had not moved.

"I...I don't know what to say John, I'm so sorry." was all Paul could think of.

John looked up at him, "The keys are still in the truck. I want to be alone now."

Paul stood hesitating, he didn't want to leave his friend, not now, not after all they had been through and especially not after what he had just witnessed on the camera.

"John, I don't think..." but John cut him off half-way through his sentence, "The keys are in the truck, leave me...I want to be alone."

Paul sighed and looked away from him for a brief second before turning back to him, "I'm not driving off. I'm not leaving you here on your own. I'll wait outside for you." Paul turned and headed back out of the house and into the silent village. The snow had stopped now and the sky was once again a deep winter's blue.

As he headed over towards the truck the only sound was the crunching of the fresh virgin snow beneath his feet, but then another sound filled the air and in the silence that surrounded him it was unmistakable.

A single shot from a hand gun split the air and as it crackled and echoed around the village Paul knew that John was now with his family.

January 23rd 2012
35° 53' 0" N, 14° 30' 0" E
19:56hrs

H.M.S. Turbulent, a Royal Navy hunter killer nuclear submarine, broke the surface two miles out from port. She had been submerged since the captain had received the emergency protocol on November 25th 2011 at 18:32hrs but now she was out of food and supplies.

The captain had no choice but head in and as she did — to replenish her supplies before heading back to her home port — little did the crew realise that they were among the very last survivors of the human race.

Epilogue

This story is of course fictional but it is hard to believe that we are alone in an endless and infinite universe with countless planets orbiting countless stars.

Who is to know that we haven't been visited before now? And indeed, the research I carried out before I started to write, shows a massive belief among people of all cultures and all over the world that they have witnessed strange events or have been visited — even abducted — and this cannot be simply explained away by conventional thinking.

How do we know that the Voyager space craft launched in 1977, which is now on the very edge of our solar system, won't in fact lead an alien race back to us as it continues for an eternity through space long after its radio transmissions stop reaching us or we stop listening?

How do we know we're not been studied, now investigated and probed, for a weakness?

And just think, if their technology is far in advance of ours how do we know they haven't perfected cloaking equipment? Allowing them to move among us without us even knowing they're here.

And to that end, how do you know, with absolute certainty, that you're not being watched right now as you read this last sentence?

Other title by Martyn Ellington:

Yesterday's Flight:

When a Dinosaur fossil is unearthed in the Badlands of America the last thing Susan Lavey expected to see as the cause of death was the tail section of an airliner.

Now together with Bruce Ackland — a chief air crash investigator — they must find out why and how this could have happened and what became of the passengers on board.

William Relford was flying to yet another meeting, but this time it was to hand in his notice, he had worked in sales for as long as he liked to remember and now was the time for a change.

But destiny has a way of changing things in ways we can't imagine, and now it was about to bring them together in a race for the truth and for one of them, their very survival!

For more information please visit:
www.martynellington.com
www.theharvesting.com

Publication by SHN Publishing
www.shnpublishing.com

The Harvesting

Lightning Source UK Ltd.
Milton Keynes UK
UKOW051811021211

183074UK00001B/73/P